Child Nazi

Studies in Austrian Literature, Culture, and Thought

Translation Series

Andreas Okopenko

Child Nazi

Translated and with an Afterword
by
Michael Mitchell

ARIADNE PRESS
Riverside, California

Ariadne Press would like to express its appreciation to the Bundeskanzleramt - Sektion Kunst, Vienna for assistance in publishing this book.

Translated from the German *Kindernazi*
© 1999 Ritter Verlag, Klagenfurt and Vienna

Library of Congress Cataloging-in-Publication Data

Okopenko, Andreas, 1930-
   [Kindernazi. English]
   Child Nazi / Andreas Okopenko ; translated with an afterword by
Michael Mitchell.
         p.   cm. -- (Studies in Austrian literature, culture, and thought.
      Translation series)
      ISBN 1-57241-116-3
      I. Mitchell, Michael. II. Title. III. Series.
   PT2675.K6K5613 2003
   833'.914--dc21

                                                              2003051887

Cover Design
Art Director: George McGinnis

Copyright ©2003
by Ariadne Press
270 Goins Court
Riverside, CA 92507

All rights reserved.
No part of this publication may be reproduced or transmitted
in any form or by any means without formal permission.
Printed in the United States of America.
ISBN 1-57241-116-3 (paperback original)

.KUNST

> The Sibyl sees
> That the world will end
> Foresees the fall
> Of all the Aesir.
> *Edda*

1 April 45   **Episode I**
Papa, why . . .? The oak table must be two meters square. Solid. Four thousand decorative squiggles. Standing in the middle of the German-Renaissance-style room together with its four huge chairs, even more ruthlessly decorated and thickly upholstered in deep red — no, that's so near to black it makes no difference. Despite its presence, and that of all the other church seating, for example the upholstered pew — in which Papa and Mama are sitting, emaciated, very pale today —, the room is still an airy ballroom. That's how big the rooms are here. And room upon room, only one requisitioned, furniture included, for those two, mother and daughter, who've been bombed out. That's how big the apartments are in the *Complex*. In the management block. And Tolko, much too weighed down for his light weight, is trotting round and round the table like a convict in all this free space.

    Pussy willow. And this Sunday's pink Easter bunny. Through a mist. As if his eyes had cataracts. No school any more. Vienna declared a war zone. Now, after the news on the radio that Wiener Neustadt has fallen, Papa-in-the-upholstered-pew reviews the situation. Come here, Tolko. You're fifteen. My people are brave, you know that. You must be brave too. But I want to fight, says Tolko tearfully. Tilki! says pale-gray Mama-in-the-upholstered-pew. For today you can still be a Nazi, says Papa, and cry over your collapse. Tolko keeps on trotting round the room and crying.

    That's enough now, commands Papa. Anatol! Hitler's lost the war, right? We have to adapt. Be reasonable. And be a man. Imagine you were a big star, a child star, and now you're a man and that's all over. Tilki, you mustn't be a Nazi anymore, says a very limp Mama. A child Nazi, says Anatol angrily and starts crying again. Papa gives Mama a look. He's grown up today, he says in a loud voice. But Anatol has a fit of the shivers; the situation's invading the house, it's not the wall map of Eastern Europe with little flags dotted all over it any longer. Will I really throw the petrol bombs I've got ready at the first Russians? Am I ready — from play-hero to real hero — the real enemy — real fright — wounds, pain, death everlasting? Wouldn't I rather assemble my telescope at last?

Papa, why did it all have to end like this? asks Anatol, bursting into tears one last time.

29 March 45   **Episode 2**
The Palm House. Soon we might not have school at all any-more. Not that you can really call it school. When there's no air raid, the few boys left who haven't been called up are sent out with the salvage squads, today we've even been sent out when there's been a full alert. We're in Schönbrunn sitting on piles of bricks, in the blazing sunshine, outside the bombed-out palm house, chipping away at bricks. Antschi grabs the cramp iron and before you know it his hand's bleeding. I had to show him what a cramp iron is and how you use it to chip off mortar. And he still believes in victory. Ultimate victory. The great turn-around. The super-weapon. If it's not the V3 which, an unperturbed smile on its lips, is taking its time coming to save us (Aristotle: moment of maximum suspense), then it'll be the V4, though by then there'll be no *Reich* territory left under its backside, it'll be the Plutocrats who fire it at the Commies. We'll all be dead and done for by then, Antschi, I say. "In the Urals there are mountains with endless tunnels," he says, word perfect in his Goebbels, he remembers everything, from the goddamn propaganda posters right down to the naked Odysseus before Nausicaa. Now the piece of skin is off. I put some iodine on

it, I always carry some since that fiasco on the Eastern Rampart (which doesn't exist). Antschi doesn't make a sound. I can just see him at the branding ceremony, going white as a sheet and collapsing, but not uttering a sound. Morgenthau wants to reduce us Germans to a tenth, a remnant that's to live by fishing and farming. PEACE is written in white on every wall, much too late. STRUGGLE — VICTORY — the last stalwarts, the ones who're christening their brats "Siren" or "Grenade," put in front of it with their stencils. Have you any whitewash at home, Fuxl, Antschi asks, I can cut out the cardboard myself. Are you crazy, I say.

26 March 45　　　　　　　　　　　　　　　　**Episode 3**
Anti-aircraft runner. Dashing along the white tunneling, night-dark by day, important, air-position plotting table round my neck, blunt pencil clutched in sweaty notebook, dashing, from the air-raid shelter through the cellars of the *Complex* to the wire transmitter. The high steps with their luminous paint — can't resist the temptation today either, and before going in I open the heavy outside door to peep up at the spring sky full of enemy planes, strictly forbidden; searchlight eyes scan the yard where luxuriant new growth is already slashed with zigzag scores of shrapnel, favorite colors green to blue, whole spring/summer ahead, searchlights already on the blue, immense day-blue, noise through the crack, but no planes. Hi, aerial gangsters. Incendiary bombs to destroy the harvest, incendiary toys unsuspecting kids pick up, incendiary fountain pens; picture of captured paratrooper in *Völkischer Beobachter: Murder Incorporated* in bold letters on his jacket, gang of murderers, fine for soldiers; warns us of devices which automatically fire a deadly bullet when they put their hands up; *Moral Insanity*,

your own phrase suits you well; shouts into the noise, in English so they'll understand, *I hate you!* Crack closes, eyes go dark, blind. On to the Tech. Office: six weeks ago, never to be forgotten for the day of vengeance, the terror raid: Dresden obliterated, Sabeff says 40,000 dead, describes how oily sludge poured into the cellars suffocating the people, like a swamp. All my wretchedness over Lisa is a splendid lump in my throat choking me, I rescue her but perish in the swamp in the attempt. Where is Lisa working now? She's been transferred to Cleaning — Papa told me — draft workers from the East are not allowed in the main Complex any longer, where Papa is giving the orders at the moment, Papa has the poison-gas course this afternoon and the evening free, if the streetcars are running again and there's no power cut we'll go the the movies this evening: *Roses in the Tyrol*, the last time it was *Women Are No Angels*, another new film tomorrow: *Heavens, We've Inherited a Castle!* Nothing but amusing nonsense now, says Papa.

Coughing from all the smoke. Time has left yellow nicotine dribbles running down from the No Smoking sign. BEWARE, WALLS HAVE EARS. Fourth thumbtack missing. See the air-wave surfer, he/ Believes the lies from the BBC. And the full series: Enemy no. 1: The devious swine/ Who cooks up rumors all the time. Enemy no. 2: The thoughtless guys/ Who pass on all their barefaced lies. Enemy no. 3: The simple soul/ Who swallows all this hogwash whole. Posters all over the anteroom, one with a high voltage warning. And the calendar photo of the observatory?? But already in the Technical Office, putting on breathless. The big red hand siren they use for the alarm. Console unfinished wood, place notebook on it, other hand leafs through plotting table hanging round neck, numbers, then target, Vienna right in middle, see visitor now, salute: officer in full uniform. Wooden loudspeaker with terribly loud buzzer. Engineer: A good lad, runs the messages. Officer, put out, something like: Doesn't he have to, then? Engineer: He's only fourteen (outraged interruption: fifteen!), it's voluntary. Officer: Is it now?! and, tersest: Sh! For buzzer noise has bowed to bomber-alert . . . large hostile formation over north Vienna. Watch out for low-flying aircraft! Another bomber formation approaching northwest Vienna. Enemy activity . . . scribbling, break-bell buzzing, emboldened by officer's exit: Sir, I can get the anti-aircraft transmitter at home, soon have it decoded, always compare it with the wire transmissions. Imitate croaky female voice: Caesar Northpole eight heading Caesar Northpole fivvvve; Eyes peeled! Lampshade! Blackout! Puffing Billy Engineer there-theres: Tell me when you've cracked it. But already, elbows jutting, well away from the Tech.

: Out in the open: the absolutely deadly planes in the unresplendent blue, their bright and shiny metal, their one Vee after the other, their unison drone. The anti-aircraft gun barks close by. Freedom like bare electric wire

Run-past of the sterile cellar passages, sections block-offable, long straight, then sudden zigzags. Bash against the rough concrete, whitewash only for the look. Damp-proof bulbs behind grilles. Signs in fluorescent paint. Open alcoves with equipment familiar from air-raid exercises: sand-bunkers, spades, fire-beaters, preventers, rolled-up hoses and blankets. A store-room the size of an apartment, also still open, glass paunches the size of little children: the *Complex's* supplies of flammable and corrosive liquids. Feel the urge to get up to mischief: dump a load; smoke a pipe. A cellar-world: when the Russians arrive, the people from the whole of the western side of the city will flee here; but it mustn't come to . . . ; The swamp is damp, the swamp is damp, it swallowed the Russkies, the whole damn' camp, granddad in the World War, the song of the Masurian Lakes, Hinden-

8

burg, gooseflesh like sealskin at "swamp," run, we must hold on till the new weapons come, Goebbels gives us hope, I've seen weapons, he cried, God have mercy on us if we use them; the bazooka alone, know all the parts, even though I don't get my hands on one till next year; the letter addressed to me on Papa's desk at home already: Army and Waffen-SS Registration Office; Papa says it's just a warning shot, Bičovski will keep me out for a while longer because of my debility. Debility!

The final sprint into another world: the peaceful air-raid-shelter company, resigned to their fate; heads bowed, nodding; heavily wrapped-up women's laps, two crumpled pairs of old men's trousers; scraped, battered shoes; the neighbors' son Joschi, no bold anti-aircraft runner he, hunched over some crochet work; hefty Trudl, father in charge of materials store; chicken-eyed, still undeveloped, but only girl at finishing tape: take last bend within a hair's breadth of bumping into her, the blush is mutual; already got planes, squadrons and single, sorted out in mind, ready to report on; report; all stare up as at pulpitpriest; casually let them have the oddest conclusion: bomber formation reported approaching from St. Pölten now disappeared. But then the officer, indignant pedestrian, appears from some alcove, barks: You, don't make such stupid reports! A bomber formation can't disappear! and wanders off, through interminable blushing and much too high-pitched Butitdiditdid, to the Tech. to sort out the muddle about the bomber formation himself.

31 December 44   Episode 4
A Lisa-New-Year's-Eve: The base is standing on a coal shovel above the yellowing marble top of a small German-Renaissance-style whatsit cupboard. At last the mouse-gray

cone-peak, burnt to a slant, is smoking nicely; behind the fragrant clouds it's bright red, bites if you put your finger too close; some of the mountains on Tolko's planets with different lava and gravity must look like that, maybe smell like that too, when they're scaring maw-gaping dragons or spidery, globe-headed manikins. The woman next door, on the other side of the wall, is also busy with a relic of the most meager Christmas of her life: after seven days spent admiring the cotton wad, cut to fit over her face and lovingly hemmed, with cellophane guards for the eye-slits and suspender-elastic to tie it on (dampen before use!), she consigns it to the oven with a final laugh: a present from the neighbors' boy, Anatol, a "life-saver" in smoke and rubble. She's an air-raid warden and the Vitrovs' advance apologies have prepared her for a sleepless New Year's Eve, even without air-raid sirens: the Vitrovs are giving a party for the Eastern draft workers of the *Complex*; didn't they come from the East themselves, once upon a time?

But now there's a headscarf, left there or lost, more gossamery than gossamer, blue, white, with a fragrance of hair, like Mama's after she's washed it, but young hair, a stranger's hair. A fragrance like Lisa herself, rich, a world full of lilies of the valley. At last Lisa is near; in our apartment!

In the middle of the noise of the good dozen dancers — no one asks for more than the bit of hoarded beer schnapps wine — in the middle of the shining teeth, a revolution of peacetime *joie de vivre*, of the Ljudmilas and Marusjas, they spoil me with songs, sayings, spells, but I want only Lisa beside me, my whole life only Lisa; in the middle of the record revolving on the blue velvet of the blue, wind-up gramophone, second time round already, though it's only eleven o'clock, the stem of Anatol Vitrov's piano stool, the fat, round seat covered in torn, blackened, penitential leather fixed with thirty-two tacks, spins round in its wide, rusty spiral tube, shoots up to the top thread from which it could release and send the ejector seat mushrooming up to the ceiling: Anatol wants to attract attention to himself. Going to play something for us to dance to, Tolko? asks drainsman Palko. Anatol can't play anything dance-to-able, never will, never wanted to, and at last the enforcer, his piano teacher, has gone to join the anti-aircraft maidens. A pain like having a tooth pulled: Palko snatches up Lisa; she snuggles into him, blue as the sky in May, transparent as cellophane, effortless as a damselfly.

Quarter to twelve. But you're not going to be sent off to bed just like that, Anatol Vitrov. While you're already starting to feel isolated from the draft-workers' defiant high spirits, from mamapapa, from the whole *Complex*, Lisa comes and sits down beside you. But Papa's there too, asking, And how's our little girl getting on? I'm even jealous of him, old, old man that he is. Fine, answers Lisa with a light laugh, as free of residue as ether. And the Gestapo? Not any more. Delighted to hear it, Lisotschka. (Papaladin, champion of the oppressed!) Will you leave me alone with Tolko? There's something I want to tell him, she asks, sweetly brazen.

The tiled stove in my room goes up to the ceiling; it's green. A small, peaceful fire makes the bed unobtrusively warm. I like a lot of pillows. This *forlorn* Lisa, this Lisa who now leaves me utterly forlorn, has suddenly been taken away from me as well. That the party is over for me at twelve, while going on for the others, is as sickening as it is standard, not a single "But" passed my lips. With the pillows, all if possible, I build a stockade round my face. I weep.

21 November 44   Episode 5
Time for Solar Prominence 21: Cold, storm, rain.

Coughing, snuffling etc. Not back at school yet, but done some exercises. No air-raid alerts. Went on reading Hans Dominik, exciting, but science fiction with too much science, typical Antschi book. He's coming to take me through the schoolwork tomorrow morning anyway. (Antschi, not Dominik.)

Went to the movies in the evening, got very sad on the way. The garden plots all bare. I still remember playing round there one summer with Maxi on our scooters. We all said, if it comes to a war that'll be no problem for the Führer. Now I've got so old. Sometimes I feel like writing my memoirs. Not a model pupil anymore, no real friends, certainly no girl, just boredom and a cold. The pain of having to queue every afternoon, all the shopgirls so tetchy, as if you were trying to steal the stuff. Just because you're a "child." The great turn-around with the super-weapons still hasn't come either. And I managed to annoy the tobacconist who insists on saying *Grüß Gott* too. I naturally replied with *Heil Hitler* and he said *Grüß Gott* again and I said *Heil Hitler* again. Something happened outside the cinema, but I'll ignore it, being of a generous disposition. True, isn't it, dear parents, if you're secretly reading my diary?

In the cinema saw *Jud Süß*, the second time. Just like the first time, filled with rage when the powerful Jew had the poor mercilessly tortured, and a pleasurable shiver down my spine when he ended up wriggling on the high, high gallows.

Afterwards the same boring way home in the cold and damp. If you can still call it a home . . . Antschi's been telling me about a solar prominence that's leapt clear and will plunge into the earth. Soon, I hope. That'll be the end of all the culture that's grown up over the millennia.

I'm slowly beginning to have doubts about myself. Let's hope it won't be my undoing!

18 October 44   Episode 6

The green card, like the silk cord delivered to an Arab's home, cannot be ignored. Guarantees toil and terrors. All year round. Sleep interrupted by the bell: night alert. Trembling, pajamas flung in a corner, and already the new uniform's filled and standing. Place giant pole on ground, swing yourself up to the top and over the dizzying rope with the pole. The non-swimmer pushed into night-cold cave-water. Burning shoe-polish tin passed on like a relay baton; to the hell in his hand come the meter-high straw hurdles under his whimpering legs. Gone the days of attendance, or nonchalantly extended non-attendance, at the *Jungvolk*, the Junior Hitler Youth: he's fourteen, life's getting serious and all the sporting and pre-military tortures of the Hitler Youth are looming. After that should come the *"Reich* Labor Service" but today it would certainly be early entry to the Führer's *Wehrmacht.*

The long gray street in the district outside the city center — not where it has the few colorful empty shops, but on the stretch with the occasional last-century cellar-workshop: STAMPS & DIES or CASTINGS, and thousands of tenement cave-dwellings without toilets or running water, and a shut-down, gray-green corner inn full of old drunken brawls in every twentieth building — brings back memories of starting school one fall, or the rapid passage of four and a half war years since the first photo of a kid in uniform. Today a father and his son are going to an office called "Area"; very silent, the son spending an unusually long time thinking about the unpleasantness in store. The father, encouraging: If you do well, perhaps you'll get into the leaders' academy. Things look even blacker to the son. He wishes something would eat up the green card. We'll just have to see how things turn out, says the father, soothing. Perhaps this letter'll help. Dr. Bičovski has already obtained the supplementary ration cards for the son, butter and milk to combat the horror of horrors — "You must eat that tuberculosis away" — perhaps he'll help him eat the green card away as well.

Now stand up straight. I'm not a German, but you're a member of the Hitler Youth. Jabs the bottom of his right lung. The son, in his *Jungvolk* uniform, marches along, shoulders back. A uniform, he doesn't know the rank yet, comes charging down the steps. Son salutes anyway, is scorned, but the father salutes as well, in his own vague way, and suggests a click of the heels.

17 October 44 Episode 7
Aerial warfare.
Tuesday 17th:
5 am get up.
6:15 off to school. Normal boring classes, the 7 boys arrive at various times. All those fit for service already sent off to the Burgenland. Harti told me about damage to industry in Jedlersdorf. Locomotive factory, automobile factory, North Rly. St. gasworks on fire, lots of apartment houses damaged! 4th class all sent home.
10:30 home. Hungary only rumor?
Radio: enemy formations western Hungary heading direction of Carinthia, Styria.
10:55 preliminary alert again.
10:58 Vienna signs off.
Wire transmission: 10:59 large formation over Lake Balaton, north-easterly course. 2 reconnaissance planes over Hainburg, heading north.
11:05 planes approaching over Steinamanger. If hold course, air-raid alert for Vienna!
11:09 air-raid alert!

— changed course for time being.

— 1st formation: continuing north, 2nd formation from Steinamanger northerly direction.

— Neusiedlersee, Bratislava.

— Single machine on course for Vienna. All rest away to northeast.

Fantastic barrage of shells!

— Concentric attack!

— Bombs, Simmering, 20th district . . .

Quiet.

— Bombs, 26th district.

Great anti-aircraft fire.

New formation approaching from west.

Bombs, North-West Railway.

Lengthy period of quiet.

— Single planes 1st, 8th, 12th district.

— Hits: Schönbrunn, 3rd district!, Floridsdorf.

— Withdrawing.

— Smallest formation approaching again!

— From St. Pölten planes now over 12th, 31st.

Lengthy period of quiet.

— Withdrawing southerly direction.

— All withdrawing.

Preliminary all clear.

13:15 quiet. We decide to go up.

13:30 another air-raid siren. No one back in air-raid shelter yet.

— Large bomber formations approaching Vienna in echelon!

Slowly people arrive.

Reported hits for 1st attack: Simmering gasworks, St. Marx, Lerchenfelder Straße, Schwarzenbergplatz, Weißgerberlände; North-West Station error, read North and Franz Josef Stations; Hetzendorferstraße, Urania Building, Wienerberg, Felbergasse, Augartenstraße, Rosenhügel, Jedleseer Straße,

Reich Bridge.
— Low-flying aircraft!
— Soon free of enemy aircraft. All clear at 14:10.
Remains of Sunday stew. Looked for shrapnel, found lots. With Papa in the main Complex. List of damage arrived there already, copied down:

Reich Bridge both sides
II   End of Augartenstraße as far as Sperlinggasse
XVII   Middle section Gentzgasse
XV Kellingg.
    Felberstr., vicinity of ring road.
X   Wienerberg
IV   Schwarzenbergplatz
Arsenal
Aspang Station
III   Weißgerberlände — Urania Building — Aspernbrückegasse
Simmering gasworks
St. Marx
III   No. 2 Dampfschiffstraße
XII Rotenmühlg.
    Gaudenzdorfer Gürtel
I   No. 13 Annagasse
XII Oppelg.
XII No. 143 Schönbrunner Str.
III   No. 14 Weißgerberstr.
    Mohsgasse
    No. 22 Kleistg.
II   Franzensbrückenstraße
III   No. 25 Hohlwegg.
    No. 2 Loweng.
XX   No. 44 Treustraße
    Gerhardweg
    No. 28 Adalbert-Stifter Str.
X   Gellertg.
    Dieselg.
XII Nos. 67, 101 Hetzendorfer Str.

XIII   No. 38 Rosenhügelstr.
XII Nos. 16-32 Kaulbachstr.
XIII   No. 3 Jägerhausg.
II   No. 43 Obere Donaustr.
     Nos. 36-42 Praterstr.
     No. 10 Rembrandtstr.
     No. 1 Czerning.
     No. 8 Försterg.
     Nos. 23, 26, 28 Ferdinandstr.
     Nos. 21, 34, 48 Untere Donaustr.
III No. 20 Radetzkystr.
XVI   Kulmg.
III Landstraßer Gürtel
     Kolonitzg.
XIX   Kuhngasse
III Nos. 8-10 Kölblg.
     No. 16 Trubelg.
V   Hundsturmplatz
III No. 3 Adamsg.

Errands: bread and shoemaker. Helped carry books down to cellar. We wanted to go to the movies, *Herr Sanders Is Living Dangerously*, but no electricity.

Candlelight. Experiments with lenses. Then light did go on.

Hungary has new government: declared total war, so no betrayal! Japanese successes: 11 aircraft carriers sunk, 8 cruisers damaged, over 5,000 register tons sent to the bottom! 1,000 airplanes shot down. 2,500 crew destroyed. Withdrawal from Greece, Jews take everyone's money away, concentration camp for children! African outfits arguing among selves and against de Gaulle.

Aunt came this evening after work!! Gas is being switched off! She's very unhopeful! In despair because of air raids etc. They say they're going to call out the last reservists. She brought some smoked meat. Bolshie talk — how stupid!

"Sleeping pills" as a last resort.

   Night: All quiet. Peace from the dogs.

22 September 44   Episode 8

What I did during the summer. (Essay) There are two things I can remember from this summer, both connected with the Complex, where my daddy is in charge of the materials store. One beautiful morning he came along and said, "Do you want to see something, Trude?" I got all excited and answered, "Yeees!" — "Then get changed and go and see Frau Policek." Frau Policek is our air-raid warden. I was going to put my dirndl dress on, but daddy gave me a pair of old and, well, let's say not particularly clean men's trousers instead. They were quite big and only fitted me because I'm well-built. Off I went to Frau Policek's, wearing the trousers and a man's camouflage shirt. She popped a hazelnut cookie in my mouth, she probably thinks I need feeding all the time, but the nut on top was already rancid. Then we went to the concrete pit, where there were already a lot of women and a few children waiting. A man in protective clothing was there as well, but in the pit there was — a genuine English bomb! *Welcome to Hell!* was written on it in white paint. "The swine!" said old Herr Dworschak, who's much too ill to work but was in the front row for the demonstration. Then the man ordered everyone to move much farther away, and hardly had I stumbled back than he set the bomb off. As he explained, it was a harmless little incendiary bomb, it didn't send dangerous pieces of shrapnel flying around, but the thick incendiary oil did spray all over the place and stank to high heaven and smoked, so we got black sootflakes sticking to our faces and everywhere. It made a roaring noise, too, as it burned, and the old wooden shed the man had put there for the fire practice crackled and spat. "It's impossible to put it out," he explained, "but you have to pull it down so it will burn out quietly and not set anything else on fire." — "With the preventer!" old Dworschak broke in smartly. "And now the sand," the man explained. "No, don't squirt water on it, you don't pour water on the hot fat when you're frying a schnitzel, do you," he said to the women. When he said "schnitzel" we all smiled at the oh-so-distant memory. As he boldly shoveled sand onto it, you could actually see the blaze getting smaller, and soon the nasty incendiary bomb was a little fire we could have made our soup on at a Junior Girls Camp. Frau Policek applauded, and a few others clapped as well.

But I mustn't forget the second event I had the good fortune to attend during the holidays. This time I did put my dirndl dress on. In the darkened People's House, the National Socialist German Women's League was showing slides of Alpine flowers. And in full color! A triumph of the German photographic industry. The pictures were so beautiful and so instructive! Rare and very small creatures had been caught on film as well, from only a centimeter or two away, and enlarged. The women also told us about age-old German customs and about the dangers they had to face to capture all these beautiful things on film.

In this summer I saw how close beauty and danger can be and I saw women willing to make sacrifices in combining the practical with the beautiful. — And is that not a woman's purpose in life?

6 August 44   Episode 9
Farmland. Aunt. Once again, on this Sunday without sirens, going through the architecture of the *Complex*, elaborate to the point of being confusing, early on this hot afternoon, through green into still greener green, into pale yellow even.

My summery youthful aunt, in the lightest of light dresses, beside me, fragrant with powder from a Paris the Germans are still just about clinging onto and with tarty lipstick. In this weather the birches, that come after the pines in the copse, an ineffective screen against the sparkling light, shelter none of the much-sought-after boletus fungi. I'm in shorts, not the black corduroys of my *Jungvolk* uniform, but horrible thin ones that flap round my knees. Aunt opines that my legs in particular are too pale; I haven't got tuberculosis yet, I snap. With infinite patience, aunt, who has a short fuse herself, puts up with the irritability of pubescent youth.

The edge of the wood and a dreary avenue to the farmland: meadows and orchards. Everything stretching out in an expanse of summer, so timeless and so finished when I want it to be young and trying things out. And that's the way I go, forward and back and jumping off the path, while the grown-up strides out, straight ahead, with the allure of a woman who knows so much about life, is so immersed in life. A tidied-up landscape, not much in the way of irregularity, not much for the pants pockets; uninteresting vegetable detritus: pieces of bark, broken-off twigs, prematurely dead leaves. A shout of triumph: one of those brightly gleaming, fantastically serrated fragments from an anti-aircraft shell, a large, sharp piece, knife-edged, it's already in my left pocket, making a bulge in my shorts. What's the matter? More new finds. Please, don't pick up the strips of silver foil, they're dropped by the planes. I've already got dozens, hundreds, I bark, with a sad foretaste of what marital rows will be like.

As always, the big barn is out of bounds. I soak it up as it looms ahead and disappears behind; the time will come when I'll ignore the sign. Did you hear Lommel? What d'you mean? I say. Lommel! The satirical revue from Berlin on the radio! I know that, I snarl, but d'you mean anything in particular? So I hear once again his Click-Clack Song, this time the verse about the unrecognisable pork schnitzels: "These schnitzels that they serve up *à la carte*, I'd say they really are DEGENERATE ART, click-clack, click-clack, click-clack." I cheer up and sing, in my deepest voice, Lommel's signature song: "The times, they say, are hard, hard for you and me, but if all we ever did was moan, wherever would we be . . ." or this, says aunt, but it's not one of Lommel's, "Herbert was lying in bed, Along with his wife, Winifred. Her butt had hardly got warm, When off goes the air-raid alarm!" She's not quite sure I've got it and repeats, "Herbert — her butt" with a little cough. I go *Oh, I seee!* and put on my stupidest face. Oh don't be so obnoxious, Tilki. Come on. Takes my arm and marches off, to music: "I feel swell, I feel great, the reason why I'll tell you straight: I just know we're gonna be friends." I've gone bright red, my arm and my legs like lumps of wood. She leaves go of my arm. You could at least ask me how I'm getting on in the labor service. Sorry! and I bow down to the ground. You ought to be pleased for me, Tilki — it's all settled, I won't have to go to a munitions factory; they're sending me to work with the mail protection unit. But why do you have to? Mobilization of labor, Tilki, and I'm not ill like your Mama. It's no fun; the senior inspector is a pain in the ass. Like me? Tilki! He suffers from dreadful complexes and he works them off on us; it's all very military; they say we're even going to get the "tank blaster," but, please, don't tell anyone.

The next building is approaching: the shed with the farm machinery. I'm important, I can keep my mouth shut. And I'll tell you something else, says the summery little lady beside me. When we go back, your uncle's going to — in a whisper — dynamite the Pont Saint Martin. I just give a duly soft and admiring whistle. Now forget I said that. I pull off some wheat growing wild. Don't put it in your mouth! And another thing: Magda comes out with all sorts of stuff at the office: "Three cheers for Otto, that's our motto." What Otto's that? My God, you've not even heard of our emperor; you know, if it wasn't for the Führer. There are lots of people in the city who've had enough, if you get my drift: "You can keep your war, we won't fight no more. Give us Hitler dead, Austria free instead." But for God's sake don't tell anyone, otherwise we'll all end up in Dachau. What's it actually like, Dachau? Never been inside — yet. Aunt, d'you really know people who've had enough? Well, things don't look too great, do they? Yes, but — my chewed-wheat mealymouth is a bigmouth again — my faith is unshaken; Goebbels's faith, too, is stronger than ever; it is a critical time at the moment, but the turn-around will definitely come. Well let's hope you're right. I shudder with the pleasant, sporting tingle of great catastrophes striking at closest quarters.

We on a ramshackle, semi-shaded bench against the machinery shed, from above the scent of wood in the August heat, a whole wall, full of brown, white, assorted creepy-crawlies. Here I am! Trifling piece of news about Inge Arenstein, still I'm grateful for even *that* mention of a girl. But what I'm after is more substantial fare, so I ask about Sonja and Sasha, where can they be scrubbing and polishing, now that Gössl's has been bombed out, the church spire fallen onto his inn? The two buxom Ukrainian girls have temporary lodgings with Grandpa; for me they've been the embodiment of the erotic in all its filthy glory ever since they paid us, namely Papa, paladin of workers drafted from Eastern Europe, a pungently scented visit. I even say in clear, I'd really love to have a girl like that. That'll come soon enough, come on, let's go down the back way, to the Trutznits. I don't want to, they're so boring. Come on. I knock her hand away. Till! If you do that once more . . . I do, so that it hurts. Now the dreaded face, the compressed lips. Beside me, without a word, down to the Trutznits' garden plot. After a while: I'm really angry with you. And after a lot of grass, the old sword-thrust: if you behave like that you'll never get a girl.

Withdraw completely into my shell like a snail, only taking in the atmosphere and acoustics of this summer with my horns, a summer that seems to be "forever," but which only seems to be for ever, one which I take for granted because it's simply there but which, because it is there, is so sensational it makes me want to shout out loud. In fact that's joy enough in itself, joy for a whole life, and there doesn't need to be anything still to come, no "great turn-around" and no girl. And in fact it's only fantastic because there's youth in it and the life that lies ahead of me and the girl, and that's why it will pass and I'll get old like the Trutznits, who just sit there in their garden grinning at each other as they wallow in their memories — if that's all — you grown-ups frustrate and embitter the only youth, the only life a boy has.

After a while: You just won't listen to anyone. Pause. Look, Herr Trutznit's giving us some *apricots*. The color and the reddish-yellow smell burst open, triggering off a thirst for apricots, a craving for food, happiness. Sitting on tottery folding chairs that sink into watered, muddy earth, the dense smell of foliage just above our heads and everywhere around. Herr Trutznit's a Capricorn, but I give a lecture on astrology is not astronomy, tell them, because the newly-read terror has to get out somewhere, about the great swamps on other planets; I accept that I'm an interesting person but you need to know the kind of person I am first, reply to it with what's left of my snappishness, with an I'm different from you Viennese and your glib, charming patter, and when twilight comes, or perhaps my twilight years, I'll write an analysis of your kind and mine.

20 July 44   Episode 10
Bathhouse. Edith sits on a white windowsill or presses a white button. In the latter case one of the colored signs over the white door lights up. She sits on the edge of a white bed and clinks her thermometers against each other in the water. Edith has another favorite now.

Across the farmyard to the bath with Mama. It's a low building full of the rich smell of clouds of steam piped over from the *Complex* boilerhouse, full of splintery fungusy sodden wood mats and large dark brown cockroaches, which share the bathhouse and flour supplies with us. The broad-hipped attendant oozes friendly unchanging warmth. She opens up the double bath. Mama and Anatol each have a curtain at the end of their bathtub and a world of room between the tubs. The sun shines down into both tubs through frosted glass. When Anatol is naked, his mother has an unexpected curtain-peep at him. Which annoys him. And she says, You're getting a bit of color back already. No more looking, he says, for today he's going to burn EDITH into his skin, down there, where it can't be seen. The idea appealed to him very much in a book about Africa, and perhaps Edith will still reply to his letter. Trude, after taking the message to Dad, sets out on one of her melancholy meanders through the garden labyrinth of the *Complex*. She feels pretty among the starveling-skinny girls of her various surroundings and climbs aboard the time machine from the slow, the boring side: a free solitary afternoon stretches out magically until it becomes a quite specific, never-heard song; all options open, you don't choose one, you mustn't choose one; you get on the other side the moment you have decided

24

on one option and start to do something or meet people; then the free afternoon is over almost before you've glanced at it. Trude prays a silent prayer before each of the flowery, shrubbery stone niches. Anatol has not even managed an E, he had forgotten about the frosted glass that disperses the power of the sun in all directions. What a brilliant astronomer! At least that way it doesn't hurt. Joschi snorts sensational stuff from a handbook on the Jewish question Father brought home from a colleague: things they'd never heard, suspected, even God — impossible to guess, almost to pronounce — is called Jahweh there and beasts are slaughtered according to ritual, they cut through the carotid artery, children of us Aryans are secretly bumped off like that as well, and the Talmud and Torah, primers in deceitfulness, and wooden drawers for divine worship, and what kind of screwy thing is a mezuzah?! And all those evil, influential Jews in the history of Europe who sucked the poor dry and advised kings and emperors and made wars. Anatol's mouth stays stuck open a centimeter. He asks Mama, who's putting on cold compresses again, about the Inge Arenstein they used to know. Weren't her parents Jews? Her mother, comes the curt reply. Trude has eventually wound her way out of the labyrinth, now she's looking forward to her hominy grits, with cinnamon sugar, astride a kitchen stool, don't crumple your dress like that! What's that? An attempt on the Führer's life?? Hands make the sign of the cross. But the wireless talks of divine Providence. Simultaneously the time machine shows the red hall of the high school, the attempted *Bürgerbräukeller* coup is being celebrated because it was prevented by Providence. Then it was full confidence ahead, to war, now even more so of course, but, says Anatol, don't take so long with the new V-bombs.

27 June 44   **Episode 11**
Traveling home. Already the dormitory had been reduced to wrapping paper through which you can knock a hole to freedom, and the other boys, who were going to stay on in this Children's Country Health Camp, turned into painted fairground ghosts, but there were still their voices, still a real, body-moving dinner, the occasional real dig in the ribs and the real stretching and kneeling in front of your locker to clear it out. A book you'd grown fond of was missing, but the dormitory thief said no and that last hotel night was too late for the thumb-screws. One last clamber up into the top bunk, one last, "Hey, how d'you feel?" and already he's stepping into his wonderful high airy home room full of dozens of impatient favorite activities, out onto the balcony rank with summer nights, bursting with flowers, over the green of the tree-tops into the holidays. No, there was still a whole compact evening to live out, hard to swallow, long to digest like the hard heavy sour rectangular army bread. Neither could be said of this morning, on which he left the camp for good and set off, joyfully reversing the gloom that settled step-by-step during the march there, on the interminable lonely walk to the station, before the train journey, interminable too, but to be crossed off bit by bit until the terminus in his home country.

A small town at 7:30 in the morning, miraculously vibrant, at least like a fifty-strong wind band, without the wind band. Every sparrow, swallow, crested lark giving voice, every corner, into which the little electric-clean Tatra Railroad car can see while it's halted, studded with small-town paraphernalia in all the colors of the rainbow. If my farewell from the Children's Country Health Camp is an absenting, that from the Convalescent Camp is a fairytale-ending: for it — for mine alone! — Sister Irmgard has organized the town, the whole camp, with pests, hangers-on, nonentities, Irmgard destroys to-the-second railroad punctuality, minutes me onto the memory of this little world, friends befriend me into an unsuspected square, cube, then all the spotlights powerlight into *one* phenomenon: Edith appears. She and I, alone in the daylight: hands are shaken, her face, for all its currantlike delicacy, hugelooming. After us nothing.

And Nuremberg really is a long way. It's all right for Vitrov, whom I meet at eight in Poprad when he transfers from the little electric Tatra Railroad to the endless filthy train to Germany: at least he'll be in Vienna by nine in the evening, getting dark, but the warmth of the day still in the foliage; for me there'll still be another ten hours to go.

Still in the dayshine, yellow: I was in the Marchfeld, north of the Danube. Vienna's not far now. In the deep-dark-green Mama will already be frying the enormous bowl of sliced potato chips. In the cumbersome, German-Renaissance-style chest my star charts will be waiting with parchmenty patience for new entries: Vulpecula, the little vixen. The Marchfeld that seems endless to us Nuremberg and Würzburg boys. Hamburg or Bremen would be a real pain! Here, hour after hour in the summery odor of straw, the symphonic grain-poem before the Strength-through-Joy operetta of Vienna. The refugees from the other countries in our compartment sing and sing, the women sounding like something out of a fairy tale, while I, a boy of nine, check out my limited knowledge of languages. I haven't been to Vienna yet, but my parents in the compartment help Tilki get over his anticipation with salami they've just bought at the frontier, a shouting Hungarian vendor popping in through the coach windows.

22-26 June 44   Episode 12
Waiting list.
0730 hrs reveille.
Room inspection.
Breakfast.
Morning colors.
Medicines issued. Will I be allowed to travel home by myself to Vienna on Friday or Tuesday?
Books issued.
1000 hrs rest cure, read *Half-Caste*.
Midday meal.
Bed.
Room inspection.
Afternoon tea.
Trembling with anticipation. Will I be allowed home? Discharges read out: Mühlhof allowed home Tuesday!
Evening meal.
2000 hrs lights out.

At 0600 hrs Thiess went home.
Midday: Scarlet fever — strict quarantine! Room 26 blocked up with newspaper, windows with plaster of Paris! We surely won't be allowed home!
Short route march.
Evening meal.
Singing.
Sleep.

Reveille.
Breakfast.
Morning colors, with girls today.
Perhaps I can go home after all.
Medicines issued.
Singing.

1000 hrs rest.
Midday meal. Kopetzki appointed *Jungvolk* monitor.
Bed.
Room inspection. Everything in locker swept onto the floor twice.
Bath in wooden tub.
Discharges read out. Despite the scarlet fever! Richter can go home!
Joy! Perhaps I can go home on Tuesday as well.
Frau Dr. Puter, check-up in day room. I have to be weighed again before I leave.
Route march.
Evening meal.
I'm called to the sick-bay. Nothing. Rudorf is released.
2000 hrs lights out.

Reveille.
Breakfast.
Free activity.
Letters distributed.
Received no. 60 from home!
Puter examination. I may be allowed home in two weeks time.
Midday meal.
Bed.
Afternoon tea.
Discharges read out. Nothing.
Cow pasture. Scrap with Kopetzki — black eye!
Evening meal.
Sleep.

Reveille.
Breakfast.
Morning colors with service.

Field exercise with girls from Mirafiori.
Learned more about V-rockets and invasion.
Midday meal: boiled greens with smoked pork.
Bed.
Letter writing. Letter 17.
Afternoon tea.
Long wait. Informed at 1600 hrs: I can go home! Goodbye and good riddance to *Ibex*!

18 June 44   **Episode 13**
Excursion to Schlagendorf. Another field exercise. I don't think I'll ever come to like these gloomy conifers. The only good thing about them is that they're excellent for tying people up to. I caught two girls from the Mirafiori camp by myself and tied them up. I have to admit one of them was pretty fat. I tied her tightly, like a parcel, and left her to the red ants. Anni refuses to join in, he prefers to *talk* to the womenfolk and skips and trips through the woods, at peace with the world. Or he identifies a leaf — there are deciduous trees here as well — and shows it to the woman who's camp leader. Or he sits by the pool and catches tadpoles, as he's doing now. I'll go and grab him and carry him off to the swamp, that's the worst thing of all for him. On the way there I'll drag him head first through the cow-pats, So you won't look out of place in the swamp, Anni, I'll tell him. The reprisals with rockets have begun. Great. Sister Irmgard was the first to bring the news, ours is in a real tizzy. We girls and the *Ibex* boys peacefully united in a fire-fever, at least the leaders are. Bomb alert lasting 16 hours in London, whole blocks collapse into the crater. You don't hear them and already they're hitting the target. Now victory's only a matter of weeks. Today we're masters of Germany, tomorrow, with geniuses like that, of the whole world. I'd

like to spend all day and night by the radio, I'd like to *be* a radio. I see the Tommies crumple and blaze up like dry straw. One of those rotten boys dragged Inge over some sharp stones. Just you wait! She's got lots of cuts and scratches, poor girl, they need dressing.

In the afternoon, after all the excitement, the nurses gave us a good bath, with birch brushes in the tub, I wanted to scrub myself, so she wouldn't hurt me down there again. A new arrival, from Jöllenbeck in Westphalia, thought I wasn't Austrian but a Rhinelander, I was very proud. But then Regional Führer Heil from Vienna comes specially to see the Viennese in the camp. He notices Vitrov right away, has him brought to the audience chamber, the kitchen utility room. Vitrov rigidly to attention, but the Regional Führer, in a nonchalant drawl, Stand easy, saw it straight away, sticks out a mile in a headwind, most intelligent one here, but we both know intelligence's not what counts. Still, if there's anything you need . . .

I stand there, red-faced and out of all my bearings, so that the Regional Führer dismisses me with a casual salute.

6 June 44   Episode 14

Rest cure. The large circle of wood-scented wooden beds arranged like spokes under the perforated dome of green sunlight. Spring at last up here, an eleventh-hour mountain spring, finally get brown, *one hour's a life*, in black gym shorts and black gym shoes. A morning spent resting in the Convalescent Camp is supposed to build up the undernourished Children's Country Health Camp inmates, quickly paint over the white of those at risk of Tb with a makeshift layer of healthy brown. Sucked up into the dome, into the spring, achieve absolute contentment, immediately followed by inevitable boredom, timeless, from all our childhoods to all our ripe old ages, to all our humanities. Followed, of course, by looks into past and future: in the cretaceous, a few days ago in the hospital, there was still E, E made you happy, friend H small compensation in the Childrens' Country Camp jungle to come, after all H is only a man, the afternoon route march will probably glow wood-yellow, wood-red again; to the sudden, childhood-old, sawdust-strewn, bark-splintered clearing in the woods, stunning with the wedgy executioner's ax and the wood-woody wood-filled hut; and some time there'll be a home — home again after centuries! — that we'll take for granted again, never been anywhere else, not been made room-leader today with responsibility increased by seven more lockers, not learned the marching song on our way home through the hot white dust to our evening milk, the song of the Boer children, *Scarce fifteen years the youngest was, Yet gave his life to save the Fatherland.* The green dome is already home, always has been, but where does this pain in his chest come from, this non-tubercular pain at a name beginning with E, true, some people are only dreamed up, root and branch. To be old in the green graveyard with the dome, which soon closes over you, as over Grandma, there's nothing sudden about that at all.

    Now, however, when you sit up, things all go round and round, over the lower dome tiles and back down to the circle of beds, no, just intersecting it and on to the kitchen, from which the commanding whistle is already antagonizing, and the hot day freezes into precise contours. "Everyone pay attention. The Anglo-American invasion has begun in Cherbourg."

31 May 44   Episode 15
Convalescent Camp. My hands all covered in shoe polish,

that's where the stench in the corridor came from, but I, unconcerned about possible losses, immediately let the Fritz, who was round the corner waiting to see me fall for it, have it all over his face with my black hands, followed by a good scratching, that'll give him something to remember me by. When you get out of Bellavista, you're too weak for the real camp, so you're sent here to *Ibex*. The girls' convalescent camp is next door and is called Mirafiori, that'll be a laugh! In the hospital we were all Austrians, mainly Viennese, here it's a mixture, lots of Fritzes. It means you learn a heap of songs. Silent night, oh what a night, Fritz and Heini got in a fight. Ten big Russkies with thumping great mitts, tried to jump them, but Heini and Fritz, sent them to heavenly peace, sent them to heavenly peace. That's one of Pannwitz's, he bites when we wrestle, so I call him Fido. That makes him really wild. He got me in a headlock until I repeated after him, Pax! Pax! my balls are made of candlewax. But — to quote Goebbels — the war is far from over. Because of the fighting and the shoe polish there was no film this evening, instead we had extra drill and a route march in the evening as punishment. A great start to my stay in this goddam camp. I'm completely shattered. If no one's owned up by tomorrow, there'll be a punishment parade and a report sent to Poprad. End of message. They say some boys, from *Chamois*, I think, have already been sent back to the reformatory in Vienna because of an orgy. The Comet came to see us in *Ibex* today, he's from *Chamois* too. He said, quite seriously, life's funny now that he won't see Edith any more. I'll beat him up and he can go straight back to see her in Bellavista. Another good one's She sits and pulls a long white thing, that 'tween two legs from a sack does swing. She pulls and pulls, out the juice flies, into a hole between her thighs. What's that? Of course, you see it now: a dairymaid milking a cow. They know what they can do with their spinach and fried eggs! Tomorrow there's supposed to be any amount of some kind of dumplings. Goddam drill this evening. A good one's Off you go, my comrade, your keen knife in your hand. Two dead from the enemy: one dies for his fatherland, the other dies for me.

28 May 44   **Episode 16**
Inge Lindner. PS. You don't need to worry about the stupid boys. We're grown-up girls and we know how to look after ourselves. Yesterday they came across the corridor again, pretending to be ghosts in their sheets and with pillowcases over their heads. One was nasty, he had a ruler with him and started hitting us with it. But just at that moment the nurse came. Everyone in the boys' dormitory got their ears boxed and no afternoon tea today (Whitsunday). There's one I like a lot. He sends me letters, but nice ones, nothing dirty. He wasn't with the others yesterday, today we ran into each other in the corridor. There was no one else around. He was glad it was me. He's very serious and doesn't make you feel he thinks you're a silly giggling schoolgirl. On the contrary, he says it's much better talking to girls than to boys. We were onto serious subjects right away and from biology we got onto love, he believes in it as well and despises the other boys who boast about their girls while they treat us like dirt. He was sad to hear we live in Bregenz, he's from Vienna. Then the other boys started shouting "Anni" and dragged him off to play Monopoly with them. Do you know Monopoly? We play it too, Eva made a board for us. It's exciting and takes hours, ideal for hospital, but we must start playing it at home when things get back to normal. Battle chess's rubbish. Love and kisses, to Daddy too, via the forces' mail, from
your loving daughter Inge

PPS: I'm eating *everything*, even porridge!!

14 May 44 **Episode 17**
Hospital Sunday. Skinny little Till, in his children's pajamas, tired, not had a good night's sleep. Now we learn why: an air-raid warning in Poprad down in the valley. This Slovakian paradise of food and sleep is starting to catch fire from the east. Perhaps an early return home isn't such an impossible daydream after all. My slippers have a military shine, the whole Sunday is spread around the room, white, divided up into its four interminably boring portions by the five meals. Meals are the most important thing, eat, eat, eat so I can get out and go home. Yet that's so unfair to our love, which just now is a bright blue ribbon Sister Edith is threading through my sheet of "Tatrapost" writing paper. And she dips the tip of her finger in the blue ink and draws an aureola of blue round a beautifully symmetrical white heart shape I've left blank, just to make Mama at home happy: isn't her skinny little Till, tucked up cosily in Bellavista at the moment, a clever boy! And now my gentle Edith should come and sit on the edge of my bed and, laughing, smudge me all over with her lovingly blue-tipped finger. Krumpf and Hainrich have been transferred to other rooms, Hainrich who woke up screaming from a dream of his brother's slice of pie which shouted spitefully, I'm bigger than yours, and Krumpf, who always calls the Slovak cleaning woman bad names, *stara kurva* and *potvara*, and was caught by Dr. Puter the last time he got into a fight with her. Lininger was told to stay in bed, but insisted on ignoring doctor's orders and getting up for his examination. "Where d'you think we are? I make my own decisions." He, too, was Puterboxed round the ears, left, right, before the door slammed shut. The cake with a glass of pink juice. Eat, eat,

eat, so I can get out! After all, I belong to the bright, Indo-Germanic, healthy side of humanity, never been to the doctor — what's this sickliness got to do with me? The last letter from home is bursting out of the envelope again; the two rectangles from the *Völkischer Beobachter* salute me with malicious, unignorable glee: "Yesterday's Air Raid on Vienna" and "This little high-velocity star, known as Hermes, came closer to us than any of the other minor planets so far discovered. It is an outer-belt asteroid that goes round the sun in a highly elliptical orbit, even crossing that of Venus. It is not beyond the bounds of possibility that at some time in the future we may become even more closely acquainted with it, if it should happen to be captured in the earth's gravitational field." I wanted to tell Edith, but she's already gone. There's the school principal at the white automatic door with the white fittings to the white balcony: the head from *Chamois* has come to visit Till! Things don't look too good, he says, the prelude to the invasion has begun with rolling attacks on the Atlantic Rampart and Italy. The decisive moment is at hand, is Till's jubilant entry with a dreadfully blunt pencil in his dreadfully grubby diary, no bigger than the palm of his hand; he never for a moment puts down the thrilling novel of this world war, only returns to reality to go to the lavatory along the evening corridor, where a nurse he doesn't know is patrolling, looks straight at his pajamas, tomorrow it's back on the scales.

8 May 44 Episode 18
Schirach. Edith. When a day, when a week starts with exceptional whistles and shouts, with a whole herd rushing all over the building, commands being bellowed, heels clicked, reports rattled out, doors slammed, in the white white of the hospital, so that the still hungry green of May

outside the usually transparent, even invisible windows is no longer there, only the interior white is left, completely cut off, the ghostly corridors full of hurry and hubbub, and even the flash and buzz of the colored lights over doors and on walls has become vicious, the nurses, the most vicious ones of course, sift and sweep through rooms and lockers, games and diaries and meager tidbits, not by themselves today, the Top Brass stalking along behind them, "A regular pigsty in here!" and everything has to be spick and span in ten minutes or else . . ., and the nurses are so terrified they yell at the boys, but things are just as tumultuous on the other side of the corridor, where the bawled-out girls blubber and fluster as they stumble everything back into order, and after all this Schirach himself is a quiet civilian. Schirach! the highest of all male and female youth leaders, on the very first common-room evening wreathed in reverential incense, now to be addressed with a meaningless-magical yelp of "Reichsleiter!' and when, asked where from, I answer "From Remeti," he even says "Splendid!" to my hair as he strokes it, yes, "Dearest Mama, There was a lot of commotion here today. Reichsleiter Baldur von Schirach was here! He was very nice;" when that's all history, Edith will sit down with Till at the white table and show him how to decorate a Mother's Day letter properly so that those on duty in the camp censor's office will like it. "The food is very good, much better than in *Chamois*. We don't worry about the future, just take things as they come: resting, eating, a little sedimentation of the blood, lung samples. They don't bother me at all now." Not a word about Edith. They are sitting down because Till is going on at the young woman about the stars, about the terrible swamps on some planets with a veil of methane over them now and then erupting in blue explosions, is going on about German astrophysics, purged of Jews, about the red shift and the Doppler principle, about the countless science fiction novels he's read, all with a happy end: the world saved and a United States of Europe under German leadership, about the dreams which the German spirit, and that of related races, has turned into reality, the triumphant development of medicines, of substitute materials, about the myths of Buna, Leuna, IG Farben, about the revolutionary German research projects of our time: viruses, protein synthesis, the secret of life, about the dream of his own electron telescope, all the time burning onto his mind the image of the little, delicate, dark, wiry girl from Berlin, still together with him after an hour on the white chairs, then Edith really has to go back to the gray Monday of all the others.

3 May 44   Episode 19
To Bellavista for a check-up. Total alienation: a bobsleigh run in spring, in spring-at-last. Used as a bypath to the valley to limit the danger from the cableway to the crossing points. Finally we giant trees, I mean we who are bright with the delayed mountain spring; may the child twisting his way downhill — does he prefer the alien world above? below?, no, everything is the too-long way home — may he commit to memory our clear-cut outline, no, our living, waving substance, ashimmer with motley greens. He would like to say something about it, fades. But then he's impelled to prefer the town below, that is to become optimistic. We fine small-town-houses scattered along the edge immediately suck him in — now he's in the infrequent town! — guide him on to the first landmark, still a very green one, gray in green: it's me, the fountain, I'm talking about; the child is to discover his thirst, break out into delight; I am cold, I am water, no, am more-than-water, that makes me especially cold and quenching and with a mind of my own, so that the child will

not be able to describe, to forget me, and the fizz bubbles up, different fizz from soda pop and less and with a mind of its own. The unfolded aluminum cup, concentric bands of metal extended until they're watertight, a work of art in itself, scoops me up for several throatfuls. With moistened lips, moist-eyed and sad, the child finally says farewell to me. Presumably to make his way to the second and last landmark, where he will likely be pierced, measured, weighed and condemned to a further indefinite term of hospital detention for his ten underweight kilograms of blooming country life.

23 April 44   **Episode 20**

A mountain climb. Gray, greenish-gray, speckled gray, everything you're afraid of, dull gray with a knife-gleam of edges in it, everything you're most deeply afraid of, slippery, no foothold, vainly clinging onto wet knives that slip from your grasp, finally a pale-green, wormwood-white bush, hang onto it for hours with the blood dripping from your hand, tightly, in white and purple spasms of pain, beneath your dangling, twisting, bellringing legs the narrow valley with the innocent Slovakian name, everything you're most deeply afraid of happens. Will you burst into flame through friction alone, if you plunge down far enough in freefall? You should never have let yourself be dragged off to *Chamois*, so close to the mountains, so close to the enemy, towering up without a break all round, they'll get you one day for sure.

So what are you going to do, now they've just announced class 5 will climb Gerlachová tomorrow? The bulbs are shining as always, the table remains a table, the other boys are making silly jokes, as always, there's no escape. A thousand images rehearse the disaster. Does no one know that will be my death, my thousandfold martyrdom?

Will no one lift a finger? Do you call that being comrades? And you, leaders, teachers, aren't I needed for something more than that? If it's plunging down the mountain that's required, you can take any stupid stone from the boulder field. But the nightmare of supper continues to loom, like the murderous cliffs and peaks, masters at waiting. This dream, unfortunately, is called reality.

Why is it I'm not ill, today of all days? Weakness, what's that? Vertigo isn't an illness. Being scared doesn't count. It'll make you strong — as long as it doesn't kill you! Oh for a severe dose of scarlet fever. Even diphtheria would be better.

Everything closing in on me. Pounding, spinning: What's the right way to climb? Face to the rock, that's all I know. How do you distribute your weight? How clumsy does the cold make you? How much can you achieve through willpower alone? What do you do if your arm's too short? If the stanchion comes away? What hurts more, to die of fear and exhaustion on a sloping ledge or plunge headfirst onto the rocks? And now Horner's telling us there are glaciers up there: tomorrow we'll be spending hours trying to keep our balance on the ice to avoid falling down a crevasse; in them you die an agonizing death, in a porridgy white, fiery cold swamp. At some point, dead tired, the boy finds comfort in the realization that by tomorrow evening it'll all be over. Then he's jerked back to consciousness by the thought that he has to get through all the time till then without one false step.

Now the peremptory whistle and bellowed commands announce it really is Sunday, deathday. You — the Supreme God barks straight at the quivering bundle of nerves — you're staying here to keep the logbook, no arguing, understood?

8-13 April 44   Episode 21

Brawlers. Easter Saturday. Now I'm in Room 23 in Bellavista Hospital. There are others here too, three younger boys: Cvirk, Zakazan, Ruländer. My fever's going down. Cvirk, a real mummy's boy, starts homesickening. He says the whole class cries when they're in their rooms in the evening. We talk about Vienna. Cvirk's crying again. He's spent the whole afternoon telling us all he wants to do is go home. It's enough to give you the blues yourself. I'd be glad to get out of here too, but I don't feel homesick. It's the enforced passivity I can't stand. I see the fever getting better and still I know that I'm going to be stuck here for another 3-4 weeks.

I've just had some ideas about my asteroid theory which immediately disappeared when Cvirk started whining that he'd sooooo love to see his little two-year-old sister again. And that's that, they're gone. Still, I've plenty more time here.

April 9: Easter Sunday! As we get up we can hear the birds singing. The light peeping in through the window is so beautiful. Easter presents: 2 painted eggs, 1 frosted coffee plait, 1 tube of fruit drops. For lunch we get: soup, schnitzel, flan. The Vienna area has been bombed?

Easter Monday. Write letter no. 3. — Breakfast: coffee and a slice of Easter cake. The midmorning snack: rolls with barley-groat sausage. Lunch: bread dumplings with meat and cabbage followed by blancmange with whipped cream and stewed plums. Then resting in bed, no talking. Afternoon tea: coffee and Easter cake. Sister Kukke's come from the camp for an Easter visit. A lot of the boys in *Chamois* are sick. Supper: Mixed vegetables followed by mixed stewed fruit. Sleep.

April 11: Boring. Book allocation: the dirty tricks of the English — the Athenia case and the tortures inflicted on the

Irish. (Set on fire as living pot plants. Buried in the bog. How cruel a nation can be!) I read out aloud, then we act it out. Ghost stories before we go to sleep: Grillparzer's *The Ancestress* and my own Mambucco. It makes me laugh, the way they quake with fear.

April 12: Boring. Acted out Mambucco: used all the bedclothes to make a suffocating swamp. At lunchtime I teased the scaredy cats, and they turned nasty.

Cowards! Three against one — one headlocks, another hits my knees, the third throttles. Wild brawl: I'm trying to stop Zakazan getting into my bed when Ruländer hits me in the face with a towel, I turn my attention to Ruländer, so Cvirk pulls my trousers down and Zakazan hits me. Impossible to fight back. But I won't blub, even if they kill me with their cowardly attacks.

Sister Bellende comes and slaps each one of us! Do I have to put up with this? Am I a whipping boy? A fine hospital this is!

Immediately after tea a fantastic punch-up. Playing stupid "signal rockets" with candy wrappers, red and green. Red — shall we finish him off? Green — let him wait. They've got an attack on me planned for the night. Show each other needles. I'll be waiting!! Jeering, mockery, insults: "Contemptible swine, Jew, liar! Disgusting foreigner!"

April 13: Slovak, Romanian, Bulgarian youth leaders were supposed to be coming. Zilch. Instead there was a lung sample with torture probe, all got goose bumps in anticipation. Cvirk whines, wishes the Commies would come! All the fight gone out of them . . . Terribly boring. I'd like to go to the camp now.

Drill was a no show as well. All-out attack in the afternoon instead. Punch Zakazan in the mug, take digs in the ribs. Cvirk with the needle. Rat on me again. Meanies: you're forced to brawl because the pack of them won't let you get into your goddam bed. You have to fight to get to lie down and then you're responsible, Sister Bellende gives you a box round the ears and makes you go without dinner. Starvation as punishment.

Evening: pulse 100! New nurse — EDITH! Potato pancakes and full-cream milk. Blood test tomorrow.

5 April 44   Episode 22
In quarantine. After you've died you wake up in a submarine, white, soundless, sealed off, dimly lit all night, completely alone. Legible from inside too: 10. And now the white is really white, my eyes have adjusted, the lighting is pleasantly bright, driving away fear, everything-but-everything is a science-fiction white, the cleanest polished white surfaces and globes, only the many signal buttons are in splendid, brilliant colors. And the longed-for drink on the white bedside cabinet. But the drink is syrupy raspberry juice and my thirst demands the wateriest, tartest iced water. The half globe of clouded glass, one of them, over the door also starts its entertainment, becomes colored, luminescent. My skin is burning again, my alien, speckled skin in yellowish and red, my eyes are full of sand again, shovelfuls to rub out, they swell closed. The swamp was here. Why's the nurse laughing. Yes, the swamp was here in the form of a man. Unbridled tears. Delight at lamps and nurse. Greedily even the raspberry juice. Since midday you've been in Bellavista. Water? You might die. Because I've 104? It comes back to me clearly. It's already lower. Is there something wrong with my eyes? You've got measles. And the death sentence puts out the beautiful noiseless lamps for hours.

3 April 44 **Episode 23**
Sickroom.
N: (writes/ fills in chart: angina, bronchitis, influenza. T 39.2/ 110)
S: What've you got?
V: (falls asleep.)
N: Everything you can get, all together.
S: And the rash? (Falls asleep)
N: (taking the thermometer out of his armpit) How should I know? Something he's eaten? (feels S's pulse; fills in his chart, repeating the figures out loud) T 38.3/ 90.
S: What have we actually got?
N: Don't keep asking me things I can't answer. Frau Dr. Puter'll be here the day after tomorrow, then you'll know exactly what you've got.
V: Will we have to go to Bellavista?
N: No way. I want to keep you here, don't I? Itching again? Come here, mummy's got some baby oil.
S: (a 15-year-old's laugh) Our baby!
N: (putting oil on V's rash) Now then. Just be glad you don't need it.
S: (older laugh) I wouldn't mind getting my oil changed.
N: (pretending not to understand the reference, continues to oil V) Are you pale! You need to get out in the sun more.
V: (punches the Slovakian pillow.)
N: What's wrong?
V: It's unfair, nurse. Spring just won't come up here.
N: At *Chamois* everything comes later.
S: But today the sun's shining like anything. Antschi (but he's falling asleep), the bigwigs are sunbathing on the veranda with the women.
N: I've told you, Schuster, you're not to get up and go to the window.
S: (with an obscene gesture) With all the women, the

teachers and the Czechs.
N: Not with me.
S: (man-of-the-world) There's women and there's women, nurse.
N: True.
S: Have you seen that Milica? (points at parts of his face) Splat!
N: Yes, paints herself up like something from a silent film.
S: But those eyes! Blue all round! Unbelievable! Nurse?
N: Yes?
S: Would you like to look like that?
N: A German woman does not wear makeup. (goes out, bored.)
S: Do *you* fancy a woman like that, Antschi?
V: That wallpaper! I could *scratch* it off.
S: Crazy, isn't it? A sickroom with black dots and lines.
V: At least we're missing geography in the junk room, thank God.
S: Poprad all we can think of, yes?
V: Joyfully we'll sing this verse
    When we're in Poprad on the train,
    Released at last from the *Chamois'* curse
    We'll never go back there again.
S: Did they ever find out who the poet was?
V: (joking) Fifty knees-bend and up before the Hitler Youth court.
S: Hey, Antschi, I'd love to have a girl.
V: But not one like those.
S: What, Milica —? (his hands make hyperboloid curves)
V: My ideal is a natural, decent, Nordic girl who's a comrade, and one for life.
S: It doesn't have to be like that. Do you know how few really stay together?
V: Then it's not love. I might as well go and jerk off in the

john. Like Dička does all the time.
S: They say his thing looks awful.
V: Can you do it all the time?
S: Well, yes, until your paw starts to hurt.
V: (Writing in his diary after his sleep: My mind is quite clear. I'm not delirious. I sleep almost all the time. Dreadful state. It's thawing in the Tatras, not a snowscape any more, everything's green already. There's a constant drip of water from the gutters and the icicles. Everyone's getting brown already, I'm the only sickly paleface left. It's so unfair.)

29 March 44   Episode 24
Uproar. Scarcely is the red blue carpet with the angular yellow cockerels that Dička "organized" for our room neatly laid out under all the furniture legs, carried off from the little hotel vestibule, which has been locked since Balagyi and his friends broke into the stores with the diamond glasscutter, when they searched the room their tooth mugs were still half full of schnapps, you could hardly see it in the dark-blue-smoke-filled air, which, moreover, also smelled of glandular secretions, the boys were lying together two by two under the heavy gray horse-blankets of a Slovakian winter-spring, taking it in turns to play the girl, Balagyi was immediately sent to the juvenile detention center in Vienna and excluded from all schools, the most important thing was that he came just at the right time to give Vitrov the final push to take up astronomy, than the whistle is blown for another thieves' parade, in the courtyard, around the flagpole, the whole camp formed up in a square, because silver cutlery, locked away, the Hitler Youth only eat with steel, has gone missing and has now, exchanged by some of our comrades for Slovakian crowns and legendary Bata boots, we are living in the peaceful land of the rubber and shoe giant, turned up

with shady locals, the police of the semi-neutral ally cooperate marvelously with our brass hats, just at that moment, out in the street Slovakian soldiers, peaceable to the teeth in their strange khaki uniforms, are playing at soldiers, Slovakian crowns, the lure of the foreign bills for pocket-moneyless, fully-provided-for boys — notions and peacetime-quality candy available without coupons in the town below, or even a rule-breaking AWOL drink in a Slovakian pub — a foreign land of peace and plenty instead of the official doctrine of a people united in privation, a small non-world-power, a Slovakian, even German "Good day" instead of "Hei'tler" and the girls all like Milica, sweet red lips sucking sweets, flirting with obscenely painted eyes — although that's no good to anyone here since the people running the place started putting bromide in our soup, Dička claims he found a solid lump, but Harti and Vitrov say that's just imagination, which doesn't mean much because the inseparable pair have sworn to keep out of all orgies and not touch their male organs until the right nice girl comes along, male organs and mating, that's from biology classes, what definitely was present in the unsalted red soup this lunchtime was fishhooks, that means the third degree for the Slovak cook, who hates us, the fifth class, the elite of the camp, we're allowed to eat in the bar now, with the teachers and youth leaders, a good thing that in our Monopoly game, home-made from memory, we don't play for Slovakian crowns but hundred- and thousand-Reichsmark notes we made from colored craftwork paper, but whenever possible we spend the whole afternoon lying round the addictive piece of cardboard investing fortunes in houses and hotels in the posh streets of Vienna until one of us has bankrupted all the rest one after the other, but in the other room, the rival school, when they play cards — sixty-six and preference — they really do play for Slovakian crowns, Sebinjak wins once again, the fifth time in a row, Vitrov has to pay up, the last 50-heller coin from all the money he lusted after, now it's clear Sebinjak has been cheating, Vitrov gives him the 50 and a cuff round the side of the head to go with it, Jeez! Sebinjak's two friends immediately hiss, and already Sebinjak and Vitrov are grappling on the floor Come on, give him one! and Yid! and spittle in the face and a cushion between their kissers into which both sink their teeth, The throat! The throat! Vitrov tries to go for it, and the writhing melee rolls, Give in! Give in! out into the corridor and across the corridor, towards the murderous, metal-reinforced stairs down, then in the evening Stifft, the old drawing teacher, drags Kaltenbauer by the ears out of our room because he swore and kicked out at little Kukke, the dry, worn-out, 24-year-old German Girls' League nursing auxiliary from Danzig, and four other towns, bombed out of each one of them; that is what you call German honor? he roars; I was an Austrian officer, and a right and a left and another right.

26 March 44   Episode 25

An idyllic Sunday in the mountains. We three: Harti, Vitrov and I. Separate rooms but inseparable friends. O spring, why do you keep us waiting? But some lovely fresh mountain snow has fallen. They say we're going to climb Gerlachová some time — I'm already looking forward to it. My violin fills the room and corridor with its harmonies. The teachers are still sleeping off last night's drink. Marvelous to have a day when you can do more or less what you like. We'll probably get meat today, I'm looking forward to that. In the afternoon the three of us will walk up to the hut — from the *Chamois* to the *Kid*. The serene beauty of the treble clef. Actually, life could be completely harmonious. Stups and Zotter have already gone out. What'll they get up to? Fighting at most. The room to myself, great, and the three of us this afternoon. Fekes, Harti, Vitrov, three names — three languages, three solo instruments playing in harmony. I wonder if you can get strings here? Harti was in the Vienna Boys' Choir, comradeship, discipline are nothing new to him, bunk beds with severe punishment for "nocturnal disturbance" when your voice is about to break. Actually, the three of us are all such good boys on the one side, and "poor soldiers" on the other. Oh, that was a mistake, missed that flat. There's Principal Tartoli having his morning cough. It's snowing nicely now. This is no good, Vitrov must get some decent color in his cheeks. I tease him that his moon-tan comes from his stargazing. We're friends, that's great. And I'm sure it'll stay that way, even when we've got girl friends. Come on, Tartoli, still at it? I'm going to have to put my bow away.

The afternoon began with a disappointment. We had hardly taken a few steps in the snow, just as far as the first bend, where you have a view out into the wild, to our waterfall — our little night music — when Vitrov said he couldn't stand heights. Harti did say to him, "I hope you never fall into the hands of our camp team leader," the new bawler-out from Germany, but we couldn't hold it against him, so we just went back. Vitrov wanted to walk down the bobsleigh run, but that was too boring for us, we went straight back to the room. Vitrov apologized. There were mountains where he came from, but he'd never done more than clamber around a few hummocks, on all fours among the red wood and the red ants, as he put it. Then he told us all sorts of exciting things about the constellations, and about the science fiction novels he reads, he just went on and on. And he had this great idea: the day will come when one country will make war by perforating the Heaviside layer over the enemy country, the region in the upper atmosphere which prevents us from being bombarded by cosmic rays. We didn't realize how late it was until we heard the whistle for cold supper.

23 March 44   **Episode 26**
Camp routine. "Early to bed, early to rise," that's us, while the lazybones are still in their stinking sacks, spick and span, "bright of eye and iron willed," whistle between our lips, we advance down the corridor, now they emerge, in their unchanged socks and underpants, merely dab their shit-smelling, bristly toothbrushes on the pinky gray soapstone and poke about in their foul mouths with them. Time for the next blast: "Line up for room inspection!" Stumbling, quaking, yakking; lockers and washbasin not cleaned in time, clothes not brushed, shoes muddy, laces different lengths and the bedmaking a catastrophe! Tear off the crooked sheets with gusto and sling them into the dirty corner — "I'll be back in two minutes and I want everything apple-pie, understood?" And "Stand to attention, for God's sake!" The next ones are already dashing into line and saluting crisply. Throws open the locker door, all the things that crowded in, panic-stricken, come tumbling out. Just wait till the holidays come, these useless clowns'll be ours for a full 24 hours a day. Another blast threatens breakfast: unsalted pink soup again with the hard army bread that only slowly softens up under its layer of sickly, watered-down malt extract.
    23. III. 1944, his name, Horrschitzer, written neatly, the inky dark-wood ruler between polished fingernails, red fountain pen in his right hand, underline with a careful pair of parallel lines, dry everything immediately with the blotter, taking care no smudges. Today's program with the blue pen: The historical development of the various Party sections: a) Foundation during the period of proscription, b) Function in

the *Reich*, c) Operations during the war. The leaders of the sections. Explanation of the expressions: "Red Front," "Reaction," "Putsch." "The Battle of the Hofbräuhaus." "Out of the swamp of so-called elections . . . the Party with all it sections." The Bürgerbräukeller Putsch. Explan. why in a beer cellar. Other parties' bar-room politics. Providence foils attempts on Führer's life. If time left: "Work instead of gold," the basis of NS economics. The perverted misconceptions of the Jewish Bolshevists and capitalists ("plutocrats"). "Democracy" — hypocrisy, parliament a mere talking shop. Only with us do the people make the decisions.

Stifft ("What is a caricature?") and Horrschitzer ("The Party and Its Sections") combine in an oversized, four-handed, two-mouthed lesson, combine with our aching backs from standing in the chairless school junk room, among the skis and a mass of indefinable old iron and wooden poles. Sometimes the mouths speak to the eyes alone. Sometimes the scene gradually does a 180-degree rotation. Your breakfast stomach, sweetened and watered, goes down and there's room at the top again, which starts rumbling for the break and midmorning snack that comes after the double-hour. Someone (still "sir," or already "miss"?) barks, my eyes flick back to reality, my ears hear again, meaningless stuff, and the hotel can't have inverted itself vis-à-vis the landscape, Poprad is still there, in miniature, down below. A hundred times more we'll see, we'll implore Poprad from up here, the fairy-tale town, from which we came up to this chamber of horrors and which we'll pass through again on our way back to freedom, when the pages of our diaries have been turned gray by longing and killing time. One day I will be in Poprad. And that day will be a real day, not the one I've imagined a hundred times, it will be a today. Recognizable in its thousand details and surprises, which I find it impossible to imagine in my unvarying wishful caricature, and in the way it will pass before my eyes and right though my body.

The head of table roars, "Allewio!" Standing round the egg-noodle table, we roar back the great feeding cry: "Alleweio! Allewio, weio, wumm. Laff widi baff widi wudi widi west, widi ran widi ban widi laff laff laff!" Then we fall on the noodles like wolves on the fold, forks on plates like arms on armor clashing. Intense munching, noodles slip down so perceptibly into your hunger, eggs season them so well, even with a cook who usually skips the seasoning, and everything cements together in a snug layer, the vinegary lamb's lettuce quenches the thirst that comes with it, and then there's water of course, marvelous Tatra water, as much as you want. But before that, line up for seconds. You can fatten yourself up like a prize pig today, if you want. Suddenly an alarming, "Everyone listen!" interrupting the bovine siesta, into which the last chewers are slipping, where sensation begins and ends at our trouser belts. "For this week —" and my crossed fingers are no use, already everyone's yelling at me, "Zotter! Zotti!" because I've just been made *Jungvolk* monitor. Damn, damn, damn — panic. What are all the things I must do? What will I be responsible for? A thousand things I want to ask leaders. But I just click my heels with a crisp "Jawohl." Must I supervise cleaning and mending, and letter-writing tomorrow, making sure every boy sends his home-sickness off to Mommy instead of playing battleships under the desk with his friend? Where do I stand during the afternoon practice drill? Do I give the commands or simply report? All mockery and moaning, all punishments will spiral down onto me. Stups, because he's not the victim, gives me a vicious thump on the shoulder, making me shrink to half size, then stands to attention in front of me with a click of the heels: "I need a shit, monitor sir!" As *Jungvolk* monitor I can't even belt him one.

Dear Mama and Papa, Great that I can send you an

uncensored letter via Nová Ves for once, tomorrow you'll get another "normal" letter. I'm fine. At first I had a little fever and was very tired, but don't worry, your Tolko will survive. We've not even been in Lake Csorba, it's still too cold for bathing, you'd have to hack your way through 2 meters of ice. I think they've sent us up here so that after the winter in Vienna we can have another winter all spring, on the model of the "Soviet Paradise." I haven't got a girl friend, we're all boys here. And no new BLUHM among the women teachers either, it's enough to make you cry. The hotel is lousy, maybe a *chamois* would like it. It'd be best at hopping up into the top one of the three bunks. As well as those there's another stinking three in our cramped room. We've got cockroaches, the winter doesn't bother them. There's a black and a brown kind, the brown ones are smaller and taste better in the bread. The washbasins are all broken, the hot taps have icy water and the cold ones boiling. We have to stand for lessons because that tub of lard, Blason, and his arrogant, painted wife, were so furious they had to take us German boys they got rid of all their chairs. Worst of all is the stupid practice drill, a lot more than at the *Jungvolk* in Vienna, half an hour of nothing but Eyes — right! Eyes — left! Fall in, in lines — quick march! At ease, ready — halt! Squad, about — turn! Squad, about — turn! Squad, about — turn! until we're dizzy. And then the singing. If we don't know their German songs, we get a route march as punishment. Zotter even said it was a good job we didn't drill with rifles, there was no guarantee his wouldn't go off. There was a big to-do today. For supper we had barley broth with worms — not pasta worms, real ones. The teachers and leaders were at the top table and we could smell their pan-fried liver. So we placed our bowls and spoons in a neat line in front of us and when the camp commander asked what we thought we were doing, our head of table said, "Striking!"

They kicked up a row, but we didn't eat anything. Don't worry, there won't be any repercussions.

Despite that, a blast on the whistle threatens a symmetrical end to the day: room inspection empties the lockers out into the dirt. Beds to be made and remade before lights out, *if* you please, until the leaders finally slam the door shut.

Vitrov was even going to ask the Beanpole if he'd enjoyed the liver, but as usual he got cold feet. In bed I told him about the Hitler Youth punishment camps. Usually it's detective and ghost stories, but tonight all the talk is of the way they use drill to grind you down (Dička with his experiences). Kaltenbauer naturally asks right away: Do they have *special* drill for them? Kaltenbauer with his "Chinese tortures" (for example underneath your collarbone or thumbing your eyes). Dička: No, in the punishment camps you just get hours of drill and physical exercises, strenuous route marches and rough treatment all the time. Could I end up in a Hitler Youth punishment camp? No, Antschi, you'd have to be a Communist, and I believe you're a Nazi. That's what they used to say to us during the time when the Party was banned, didn't they? See, sings Dička, the way the sergeants drill us (to the tune of 'O wie werd ich triumphieren' from Die Entführung, Dička on the right, Vitrov on the left in a headlock, alternating with kneeing him in the balls, Grab his nuts, hold them tight, pull the left below the right) Sure the bastards want to kill us, Blood drips from our hands and knees, hands and knees, Blood drips from our hands and knees. And they really sing that in the punishment camp? I ask. Dare they? They've nothing to lose, I say, some have GCP or even the Soviet star tattooed on them. What's GCP? I ask. Do they do the tattoos with a branding iron? I interject. It's just German Communist Party, I explain. Ridiculous to ban it, it'll always exist. In

Russia they died for a watchword: Nebuchadnezzar — ne bog a ne czar — Vitrov understands: no god and no emperor. He likes wordplay, the whole of literature could be wordplay as far as he's concerned. That Christian Morgenstern, with a name like that he must've been a Jew, I say. Have you lot got a slogan like that, Kaltenbauer asks. Dangerous question, but Dička refuses to get worked up. I'm a *Jungvolk* platoon leader like you, he says. I just meant . . . you seem to know a lot about it. Go fuck yourself, says Dička. Then he goes silent and starts panting over his prick. Madame Rosa? Madame Yvonne? wonders Vitrov. He's learning, but it still fills him with contempt. He'll love pan-fried liver for the rest of his life, you lot live in another world. If you would help to build the house, o stone, We first must carve you into shape and hone. The rather silly verse was on the noticeboard in glorious Gothic script. We first must starve you down to skin and bone, Vitrov would like to have the blushing nerve to tell the leaders to their faces. Harti, Schaffer and Pipsqueak Piebel are already fast asleep, the constant roar of the waterfall, straggly as a billy goat's beard, comes in through the single-glazed window, Vitrov can stretch out into the map of the Slovakian landscape, into his fear, alone now with gigantic swamps.

20 March 44   Episode 27

Waiting outside Bodenseil. It's not true that this unwanted, burdensome, apathetic setting-off for an uncertain fate right in the middle of the great, gray-white cold and right into the middle of it, into the cold of unexplored, east European mountains only superficially civilized by small towns and vehicles, this enforced departure at the wrong time, a time when one had at most just enough strength to arrive with a last gasp at the destination to fall into a deep, leaden sleep, like the brown bears they still hunt here — it is not true that this is happening at around four o'clock on a darkening afternoon to a member of the German *Jungvolk*. It is endless years ago, my parents are close by, Miháiu still nipping all around my badly sewn-up heart, where hours are waited not for *Jungvolk* luggage, but for the last bus that has not arrived, the escape bus out of the snow into the snowsnow, perhaps it's already been requisitioned or redirected to hell with its first complement of passengers. But Anatol Vitrov holds the big star atlas between himself and his parents, that's the thing he'll protect longest of all when they come to massacre them, borrowed till we meet again from the old engineer in Remeti, admired by and admirer of *Tolco*, hours of hypnotic reading with all the formulae of spherical trigonometry, not understood, but their meaning sensed, why do you need to know that xi and eta are Greek letters when the meaning of the celestial coordinates determining the position of each star, its precise future path, is clear, at any given moment you can say what the position of the fruit fly on the penknife-scored apple is. Then in some meantime or other the dimlights and shadows of the endlessly flitting-past landscapes start to kinematograph, somewhere there is warmth waiting and the second Remeti, no, the *Chamois*, thick kasha hot as sealing-wax, no, German-Slovakian pease pudding, beside the straw-filled sacks with my parents, no, beside roachy bunk beds full of *Jungvolk* comrades dully brooding with me, at my destination. At a destination that is just the most timidest beginning of a return to Vienna that will take months.

20 March 44   Episode 28
The Mountain. Horizontal travel. This stupid stop's over at last. Like yesterday, when we arrived at the obstacle: ten

o'clock in the morning, station outside the town. Wasted 24 hours. Wind gusting through. Endless wait for the train to take us to the next stage, a few months of camp. We're feeling like giving a push to get back to Vienna and on with our real lives.

The paltry, late-winter-gray waiting, waiting with nothing to look forward to, still dripping with sleet-flakes in the sunshine: going on tedious detours away from spring towards the Tatra winter is forgotten because suddenly The Mountain is there.

Towering straight up from the station, facing us, dragging thrown-back heads upwards: the clearest green, unwelcoming, bitter, freshly washed, probably only 200 meters high: another world, entirely alien, as if the moon were knocking at our door. And on every one of those meters, to which our eyes are steeply drawn, there is life going on; already I can be seen out walking with Mama and Granpa on all fours, height-terrified; they point out the purple, midsummer plants covered in the brown glue insects get stuck to; Papa's car is grazing down below, where the mountain suddenly towered up after a bend in the track; even the turf of the lowest slope, heavy with the fragrance of August herbs, I grasp with all twenty fingers; heading for the uptilted horizon with all its unknown flowers.

Another possibility is brought about: it is around 1.30 pm, a *Children's Health Camp* boy is standing by himself in the last car, taking the salute from the landscape marching past the train, a strip of meadow, trees beyond, for half an hour, an hour, two hours, a fresh, gloomy, deep-frozen forest edge, conifers, conifers, then, some eventual time or other: Poprad, where all the waiting really begins at last.

19 March 44   Episode 29

In Zilina. We were sitting in the compartment with expectant expressions on our faces: Dička, Vitrov, Schäffer and me. The window was open and we had been stopped for quite a while at this unpleasant station. What we would really have liked would be to travel right through to Poprad without having to change. The train moved forward a short way, then stopped again. The leaders' whistles sounded along the corridors: "Everybody out." We quickly put our coats on, grabbed our suitcases and got out with our burdens.

Our welcome to Zilina was a lump of bloated, sooty snow splattering down off the roof. A voice squawked, "Quick march! Line up at the station! At the double!" The actual station was a long way off. We were sweating, despite the cold, because we had to carry our cases.

There we waited for half an hour before we were marched off. We had to stand in the snow without moving. The snow was an amalgam of soot and dust which went right through our shoes.

We picked up our cases and marched a little way. We put down our luggage in the long station concourse, we didn't have to carry it any farther. Then we marched to a hotel. The funny lighting (alternate red and green windows) put us in a strange mood.

I was put in a room with boys I didn't know at all. Then we were told we had to go back down to collect our suitcases. It was bitterly cold outside. In spite of that, I was sweating as I marched up the three floors with my heavy case. And the same again. Dripping with sweat, my hands filthy with soot, I was going to sit down. Only then did I notice that the room contained the following items alone: one wash-basin, without soap or towel; six two-storey bunk beds; one door and one corner window. I attempted to fish a towel and soap out through the crack between the suitcase and the lid. In vain. I "washed" myself and wiped off the dirt on my handkerchief and rucksack. We sat down on the beds. That was it for the day? The twelve of us sat there, bored stiff, waiting for our food. I imagined it must be late in the afternoon.

At 12:30 the whistle sounded and we ran downstairs. There was a pleasant smell of goulash in the room. But all we got was some horrible pease pudding. I noticed that most of the others immediately lost their appetite as well. Despite that, I ate up everything, even the lumps of fat and the disgusting strips of all kinds of animal skin that smelled off.

Afterwards one of the leaders gave us a little talk. We were to rest for three hours. We collapsed onto our beds, fully clothed. The leaders came round to check. Those three hours were exhausting, after all our exertions and running about it was terribly boring, we had no books to read.

Three blasts: snack time — half a cup of herbal tea and two slices of bread, one with margarine spread as thinly as possible, the other with a similar layer of jam.

After our snack the group spread through the rooms and into the lavatories, permission for the latter being granted insofar as the lavatories themselves permitted, since most of them were full to overflowing.

I very gradually began to feel ill. It seemed as if the houses were moving past the window, then I knew we were in the train and moving.

18 March 44   **Episode 30**
To the East . . . No, the blacked-out carriages, exceptionally with a cargo of German boys in need of feeding up in Tiso's allied Slovakia on a line usually closed, ie restricted to traffic related to the war effort KEEP THE WHEELS ROLLING FOR VICTORY, are not yet rolling at 8:13 pm, even though

everything's clunking and hissing VIENNA OSTBAHNHOF before the scruffy goodbye note has been handed down to his dear parents (aunt was forgotten) and Red-Riding-Hood aunt says, What a deep voice you've got today. No, it's not because of yesterday evening's suitcase-packing-with-air-raid-alert, nor for some reason or other even the hour this morning outside the school with the hard-handled snowpusher blistermaking on gray woolen, red-skinned bemittened hands. But now, at 8:15 pm, after an ignored embarrassing, "One last kiss!" and some manly-minimal handkerchief-waving they finally start rolling. Relieved, Viennese pubertarians of all sizes drop back into the hard compartment, into the excitement of the great journey.

But all that happens is that at 9:30 pm not a single Slovak crown is sold to them at Marchegg, despite the fact that they do not leave Devínská Nová Ves until 0:48 am, at 1:30 am tea is served to the night-yellow ghosts in Bratislava, at 1:50 pm they stop between stations, when sleep overtakes them, to be broken off for good at 5:30 am because they are moved, saddened, gripped by the occasional, lonely, blackish-green, grayish-black farmstead in the halflight blackness, halflight dark green along the Váh, shacks with shaggy roofs reaching down to the ground, finally the Váh itself, flowing along, so uselessly lonely, in the night — and it is as if all bridges are finally burned behind them when geography exclaims, "The Beskid Mountains are visible!"

Fall '43   Episode 31
Evening lesson. Bluhm. What's the matter, Antschi? The matter is, I've finally got my terrestrial telescope and it's the evening phase, I could use the telescope right now to observe a very earthly event, and I could well do without the evening

phase, if you have to set off for school after lunch, that's the whole day gone and you're fagged out and everything's just starting, the only light in the whole evening phase is Frau Bluhm, our German teacher, my Frau Bluhm; I am proud to say I loved Wagner before she came, in the greed-filled goblin's cave I cast the shattered sword anew, like telling your fortune by pouring lead on New Year's Eve, mine came out like Frau Bluhm, the very image, a cherry-sweet revelation, and after my essay — me with a model essay "Remember Stalingrad!" that was read out! I really only have Frau Bluhm to thank for that — my whole mood is heading more towards twilight of the gods and yesterday evening I caught myself taking the detour across my newly discovered, horrible rubbish swamp and almost trying it out, would I plunge head-deep into the thick black clayey dragon's blood for my Bluhmhilde, to become one ash with her in the flames of Valhalla, laughing the Commies to scorn?

Sumthin' the matter with your Bloomie, Tolko? I hear without anyone asking. Erecting the image in the terrestrial telescope increases the length of the tube by four times the focal length of the inverting lens, but all that, if you look at it closely, is superfluous, because even the astronomically inverted image of the cardboard dinosaur in the equipment cupboard would have smashed me to meteors; now the gloomy yellow lamplight on the desk, the bespattered sitting machine graygrimed with the years, but the design of the telescope on the gray, blotch-absorbing paper, with the chipped, finger-inking ruler is spotlessly, no, dazzlingly white: now I have the telescope on the day I lost Bluhm; recently she's been praising my German essays more and more, even smiling at me, but she praised Osman, the oldest in our class and author of pretentious poems, in a quite different way, and today, through the wide crack, the result of an old brawl, in the locked equipment cupboard I saw in the clear light my blonde, bright-bosomed Valkyrie, full of good, ripe female flesh, lifting up her skirt high behind and Osman, my recent humiliator with that blasted Einstein, all star pupil, all lover, all body and nothing but body, bronzed as if from the colonies, hard-muscled like an oiled ju-jitsu fighter, with the dude's magnificent, black-greased, thick razor-cut hair, already stuck deep inside her I imagine; I fell into a slight swoon from all these mixed feelings and realized for the first time amongst all that what a splendid thing a bottom is, which until then I had seen merely as a seating arrangement, a piece of lavatory equipment, a source of insults, and sensed what a happening is as Osman's dude's toiletries and my Bluhm's Houbigan de Coty, subtle and sophisticated but unimaginably whorish coming off her hot body, mingled in unruly swirls right underneath my nose. O comet, come down now and destroy Valhalla, I screamed inside my head and commanded the waves in my trousers to subside and not join in the celebration of my tragic love.

Sumthin' the matter with your Bloomie, Tolko? But I have my terrestrial telescope and go to the john after the physics class like a good boy, I will not betray my Bluhm, I say, moist-eyed, and turn into a hero shuddering with emotion. Leinsamer is standing at the urinal and gives me a push. "Me first," he snaps. "Just because you're a platoon leader?" I snarl back. "Rubbish!" And with a dirty laugh, "Might is right." I'm in such a state today I could smash his skull in so it bursts into pieces, each one with a bit of stupid, might-is-right brain sticking to it. If I had some detonators on me, today I'd set off the whole box in the palm of my hand, as I didn't do during the trial of courage in the lavatory, all the fizzing white heat at once. So, after all, you have to let Vienna's marvelously ugly, tenement-district autumn wind calm you down, let it accompany you through the darkened streets with the cheering little dogs cats elephants molded by the light on shabby coat-collars to the blacked-out, firewood-rumbling streetcar, finally delivering you home to your still-absent parents.

Recently this absence, a valuable possession, gripped me. We're at the movies, warm up the potato pancake pieces — like hell I will! I run into the bedroom, onto Mama's bed, tear the clothes off my body, slip in between the sheets, at least guaranteed thoroughly non-chaste, rummage round in the bedside cabinet, quickly find the little bottle of perfume, not Houbigan but something similar by Coty, take out the rubber stopper and dab nose left, nose right, mouthhole, male organ — I still use the word from sex education — and then I have my Frau Bluhm for the one and only time in my life. And how! But before I have her fully, I dash in alarm to the john clutching my foreskin tight. Mama thinks there's a strong smell of perfume, but Papa says, come to the study, there's something I want to say to you, and as I come to the slaughter, with cordial ceremony he offers me his renaissance-style master's chair, it's all purple ink and spluttering pens here, "You know you're growing up into a man, Tolko," — "I know," I say eagerly and with all other feelings together as well. "You'll have been told everything at school, thank God, but I'm talking to you from experience. I'm sure one day, like all boys who haven't got a girl-friend, you'll masturbate." The blood pulsates by the bucketload through my body. I carve the whole chair anew. "But I advise you not to do it too much, otherwise some day you'll make a fool of yourself with the ladies. Come here, see what this man's written." I can't tear the book out of Papa's hands and I can't read the name. "It's probably banned today, but it's very intelligent." Papa says he was given it recently by a woman asking him to put in a good word for her, oh yes, that still exists today and it's nice if, even without belonging to the system, one can help people a little just through one's professional position. I'll explain that to you later, you smell like a man already, but you're not fully a man yet. Banned, oh yes, there are lots of books that are banned today, the whole of Dada, for example. Come, I'll show you what your Führer has to say about it. I immerse myself in *Mein Kampf*:

It is true that in earlier times there were occasional lapses of taste, but in those cases it was more a matter of artistic aberrations, to which posterity could at least allow a certain historical value, than of products of a degeneration of not just the aesthetic sense, but of the mind itself. In these latter the more obvious later political collapse first announced itself in the cultural field.
Bolshevism in art is the only possible cultural mode of existence and aesthetic expression of Bolshevism itself.
Anyone who finds this puzzling need only examine the art of those happy states where Bolshevism now holds sway. He will be horrified to find the diseased creations of the insane and the degenerate, with which we have been familiar since the turn of the century under the names of dadaism and cubism, installed as the official state-approved art.
Sixty years ago a political collapse of the extent of the one affecting us today would have appeared just as impossible as the cultural collapse which first began to appear in futurist and cubist pictures after 1900. Sixty years ago an exhibition of dadaist "experiences" would have simply been seen as unacceptable and the organizers would have ended up in the lunatic asylum, whereas today they even preside over artistic associations. At that time this plague could not appear because public opinion would not have tolerated it, nor the state have stood by unheeding. For it is the duty of the leadership of the state to stop the people being driven to insanity.

"That's enough." Already the book's gone and Meyer's Encyclopaedia opened. "There, read that."

Dadaism, a movement in art which started during the World War and caused a stir until about 1921; rejecting all hitherto accepted aesthetic laws, its ideal was the unrestricted arbitrary power of the artist's personality, often seeming to be a mockery of existing trends. The name comes from "dada" the first sound a baby articulates, and which dadaists called the highest, most direct revelation of art. Elements of cubism and futurism also influenced dadaism. The —

"Well, Tolko, now you know, yes?" Actually, all I am is confused. "D'you know, the thing that irritates me about you Hitlerites is the way you're always saying JAWOLL! instead of just "Ja." In the Slav languages JA means "I" and VOL means "ox" — or "idiot."

Fall '43   Episode 32
Neighborhood roamings. The *Complex* no longer holding what's wanted, your expedition range is extended. Not into unknown territory, but to that already known-but-unseen from must-journeys. Thus the streetcar route to school is repeated on foot at nonschool times and with variants down side streets or overflows into green spaces, also to small, dark factories, which naturally attract your attention. One sends shivers down the spine with the stench of burnt hair you can smell from miles away. In one there's a grinding and a splintering, and mountains of green and white glass chips are thrown out towards you. Accompanied naturally by the gloom-gusting autumn wind, all promise of summer gone, sometimes howling and with flurries of rain. Everything's so completely over. But then you get lost, and the gloom is gone with the path, and far and wide it's damp-green and forbidden and the next step is dragging shoe and stocking and foot down into the blackly wobbling oil; one step back and another in the direction you thought you came from and oil again, knee-deep this time. A hundred landscape shards, wishes, schemes of escape — and, above them all, set to music by the oily gurgle of the storm blast, a scrap from some

adventure yarn was suddenly there to horrify for nights on end:
Dalai-Nor,
Dalai-Nor,
the man who treads its mossy moor
will never come out, nevermore!
Dalai-Nor!

Fall '43   Episode 33

A German lesson. The yellow sun does not fool us, it's the school windows it's warming now, not the surface of the swimming pools. It evaporates the brown bitumen of the school floors, the acrid smell goes well with all the school urine and the rag-must of the gray blackboard duster. Its slanting rays are shining on the outside-left desk in the 2nd row too, warming one corner of the gray exercise-book cover entitled "Vitrov's Star Atlas." The good smell of warmed paper, even cold clean wrapping paper has it, though now, during this war, mixed with the moldy stench of the dust we breathe in at the same time, hovers over the snaggy, dirty desklid, making our mouths water, our stomachs rumble on this early morning. The title on the exercise book hardly legible, a mixture of the old sloping hand, trotting along to the teacher's dictation, and the new upright one, testimony to his awakening self-confidence. The thick, bold "l," furthermore, could be any number of other letters, isn't Vitrov at all, one last relic of friendship from and for Schlesak, slowly fading as the girls begin to dawn. Thirdly, his self-tormenting concern that a stroke might be too faint or not neat enough has made him go over some again, or even a third time.

"Osman, Harti , me — now stars of the first magnitude" is written on the first page of the atlas. "Because of girls, the most important thing no longer football, fighting, swearing. Take over power through intelligence, jokes, dirty talk, manners, dress, music, experiences, coolness, enthusiasm. It's not the footsloggers who rule now, but the officers, with whom I belong, at least in terms of intelligence."

Separate pages:

OSMAN: "Star of first magnitude. Oldest of us all, joined the class because repeating year. Not for first time. But very intelligent. Dude, but first explanation what dudes really are and want. Despite political differences immediately shook hands as token of respect of one gentleman for another." "With his hair-style, coolness and knowledge of banned swing he's already turned our previous elite into followers, in particular the sporty types, loudmouths, bullies. *Note: What is this thing? This is a swing.* They say he has a real secret club, for a joke we call it OGHC — Osman's Girl Hunting Club. Where they smoke, drink whisky and get up to some pretty heavy stuff. He claims to be a poet too, but I find him too pretentious. In something that he read to us, full of overblown feelings and distant lands, there was even the word Picasso. There are words you happen to have heard God knows where which make you blush."

HARTI: "Star of first magnitude. Joined us from another school. Very serious & intelligent, at the same time capable, sensitive, natural. immediately became my best friend." "Thought a lot about Harti-Schlesak difference. Now girls are what Schlesak used to be for me, that is, what one girl will be. Harti's waiting for one like that, he's not even going to jerk himself off until then. Could talk all day. That's how it's going to be with my girl. We immediately made an alliance against the decadent influence of America and Osman."

BLUHM: "*Supernova.*

Nova is the astronomer's name for what appear to be "new" stars which suddenly shine brightly in places where previously there was only a very faint object, or where none was visible at all. In some cases the brightness of these "Novas" can increase by a thousandfold within a very short period, only to return to a dimness which means the star is once more impossible to observe. Measurements taken during observation of such stars has revealed a striking regularity: almost all attain a maximum luminosity which is approximately 25,000 times the brightness of our sun. There are, however, conspicuous exceptions, namely stars whose maximum luminosity is many thousand times greater than that of the regular novas. The designation "supernova" is now general for "new" stars of exceptional brilliance. Supernovas have been observed, which in the course of their brief increase in intensity reach a maximum of more than 300 million times the brightness of the sun. In any single galactic system, such as the one containing our Milky Way, the appearance of a supernova is a rare event, probably once every thousand years. (Copied out of the *Encyclopedia of the Contemporary World*, 1940.)" "Should not really be in the star atlas because she's a teacher. But she's also a friend. I got Wulsch, lout and joker, once my tormentor, to write on the board with a piece of chalk wetted so can't be rubbed off, "Gerti Bluhm we love you." She went pink, and when she found it wouldn't come off, she didn't know what to do. Confession: there's something wrong with my self-confidence as long as I can't tell her that straight out, without recourse to the oaf and his tricks, can't tell her to her darling face among lots of kisses." "Instinctively she took her revenge through my homework: a bright person like me shouldn't have such crabbed handwriting. Resolution: I'll stop going over letters again. And my Bluhm shouldn't be written with the Schlesak "l," I'll invent a bright one of my own."

The summer's-past-and-gone sun, the school-from-now-on sun highlights Lovodik's yellow, perhaps even chemically bleached strand of hair, throwing wasp stripes across the dais where, even after the bell has gone, though ready at any moment to plunge down peregrine-like under the blazing eye of the Valkyrie with the register, Lovodik sings, imitating instruments and accompanied by contortions and faint applause, *ex cathedra*

    In the bar in New Orleans
    Did you hear those ragtime tunes,
    See the black girl do the shimmy
    Twist and shake her naked belly
Unthinkable in pre-Osman days!
    See the big buck do his stunt,
    Give her one right up —
Enter Frau Bluhm. And first of all, after "Hei'tler!" and "Hei'tler!" of course, the prepared lamb is invited to the slaughter: Vitrov has to give his talk.

    Vitrov's topic is astronomy, everything from the basics to the latest developments, and he gets carried away, speaking more and more rapidly as he enthuses about the origins/end of the universe, until he realizes he is not going to be able to bring it to a conclusion, even if he had the whole of the double period. So he pulls the ripcord and floats down into the more sober stratum of astrophysics, expressing the hope, by a false analogy with the supermicroscope, that the world will soon see an electron supertelescope, which the Germans will also invent of course, if they aren't doing it right now, thus showing up certain absurd theories, such as those of the Jew, Einstein, for the ridiculous nonsense they are. Osman stands up, raises his arm and says, before he's even asked, "Objection." "Yes?" says Vitrov, politely. To use race as an argument against a great physicist like Einstein is unscientific. If you can disprove the theory of relativity, then go ahead; I don't know enough about that kind of thing. Bluhm gives Osman, all noble, well-controlled anger, a

Valkyrie look, the two of them go well together. Vitrov feels his thoughts turn to paper that is slowly being crumpled up; or: the Hitler ring breaks and Vitrov falls flat on his face in the sand of the arena. You chose too broad a subject area, Bluhm says to little red Antschi, before proceeding to the next item on the agenda: the German dialects.

Vitrov reconciled. For he hears that with his extempore sample of Viennese dialect he would be considered more German than Austrian: hard attack, pure, short vowels, brief sentences, no singsong, just meaningful emphasis, abrupt termination. For a second time today he goes red, but this time with pride: with his inadequate adaptation to Viennese, with his false Viennese — the years of mockery from his classmates are not forgotten — he is, as testified by a Valkyrie, as good as a member of the master race, a Berliner, for example; brisk of speech and brisk of action, brisk at lying down, brisk at getting up, changing, gym. None of this swinging, chewing-gum charm, I'll always come straight to the point. And I'll be loved for it, am loved already, my status what it always was, a model pupil in the country — not yours.

In the sad yellow sun of school bondage we are given the story *Blind Obedience* to prepare in the sad yellow sun of notplaying and notbeingbored at home. The title is briefly explained: in this war we should *not* obey like the blind, but like men who can see what they are fighting for, can understand the leaders' thinking; not the way the Yankees mock us: "Left, right, left, right, Hitler knows why we must fight, and America's a long way away." A good transition to the conclusion of the German lesson, one of those short, brisk addresses by the leader of the Hitler Youth, Arthur Axmann, from our reader. Lovodik makes a slip of the tongue when he reads it out loud: "We of the Hitler Youth pledge ourselves to father for the fightland to the last drop . . ."

End of June '43   Episode 34
Negro drawing. It's clear we're heading for the summer, for the summer that's just beginning, with ammonites, belemnites and all the tempting, dry, limestony snailshell stuff, those uncomplicated, warless fossilized things, half creatures, half things. In city squares that cough up white dust the school barracks are celebrating the last day of school. First of all, however, we have the oily, slightly curdled Indian ink with the scratchy drawing nibs on a much-too-large sheet of paper, but this time it's fun, an unexpectedly high-spirited outpouring of negro fun: a brilliant idea, even if it was the drawing teacher's, on the *Reich* curriculum theme of "Germany must expand," this kind of expansion is right up our street, all the things the negroes, as crooked little ink-stick men (and women!), get up to in our future colonies, a real bit of summer fun this is going to be, the fifty minutes are far too short, please, we want the film to go on as they sit at the potter's wheel, stand at the forge, disappear into a hut (Dička whispers, and not even very quietly, what the negro women shout as Goebbels arrives in our newly acquired colonies: Quickly, shush, all the women hide in the bush) the way they daub black ink over each other's black inky faces and drink crooked black inky water out of crooked black inky jugs — it's a free interpretation, and is it not also a little bit contrary to those Nuremberg Laws we've just been swotting up? I believe it's not quite so bad with gypsies and negroes as with Jews, and in the colonies the negroes can be as black as they like, we love them, Papa is not a member of any National Socialist organization, but he is in the German Colonial League, he'd even move there with us after the victory, the eternal adventurer raising a *Complex* from blueprint clay and pottery shards, I produced a kraal as well, for their crooked black ink-cattle, the badge has a few stars, more modest than the

Yankees, I'll manage it, how quickly it's all over and there's the dusty street and the streetcar with the open platform to jump up on, into the dust and the green and me in my short red loden jacket, I think I look great in it, and, yes, really, everything's there, ready, open, summer, how free we are, free, imbuing all our vigorous work, ranging free out in the open air with magnifying glasses and grids and figures; a century, an eternity of holiday begins: free!

June '43   Episode 35

Yarrow. Yarrow is in flower from June to October. The best time to pick it is when the flowers first appear. For that reason I have chosen to place this episode in the last month of the school year, June, although the boys meeting in the pitch dark of early morning would suggest October.

The face of yarrow. Memorize it so the wrong — useless, poisonous — thing isn't gathered. Are they all looking for yarrow or only him? From now on eyes for nothing but yarrow. Impressive filtering out of the landscape he's unfamiliar with anyway even though close to school and in solar-eclipse darkness into the bargain.

No song is sung. Only yarrow is sought. The target-white of the flower makes the surrounding area blind-man's-blurred, even after day has dawned greenish-yellow, with only occasional random sharp edges sticking out.

Incredible! Everything that's seen — that's blinded — is only a few hundred meters, later a few kilometers, from the school; grown-up, every area will be a colored-in map with no blank spaces. The teachers are different people, lead, know, can identify everything; collect different stuff, not squatting down so often in the wet, dry, moss, sunshade, winking at each other.

A turning-point in his life: Dička decides — on the

strength of his powers of observation expressed in having learned the Vienna telephone-disk code IFABRUMLYZ off by heart — that someone who thought he was fat-therefore-dumb is intelligent and therefore likeable, gives him a friendly greeting, "You don't *have* to be dumb," but he forgets to finish the rye-flour pancake he's just bitten into and simply stows it away in his rucksack, without its wrapping.

The herbs collected during this operation are spread out in attics to dry.

May '43   Episode 36

Granma's funeral. She was always part of our world, always part of our lives. Of course I still see her, as I did every day. The way I will always see her, or will that slowly disappear because she isn't there any longer? No longer anywhere in this world, no longer with us and soon will be spoken of less and less, you can tell from my great-grandparents, whom I never knew. That's right! — from my other grandparents as well, who've just come back to mind after a four-year gap (*four years ago*, family tree at school, Certificate of Aryan Descent from the Ministry of Genealogical Research); the dead as a dead loss!

"It'd be too much for him to go to the (DING-DONGDINGDONG) with us." Let them think that, I'm happy to stay at home, in the *Complex*, in this greenest-of-green, most luxuriant month of May *where*, in the artificial natural woodland at the top, the pines are just shedding the crisp little light-brown hats, husks sticky with resin, from the new, bright-green brushes, bristle by bristle, you can hear the rustling on the warm May nights when we go for walks through the woods and farms, through the smell of pigs and hay, of cooling herbs and fruit-tree blossom, of pine resin too, of course, just the three of us, aunt, Mama and me, while Papa's still working on his reports and uncle, his nerves repaired, is back deep inside enemy territory waiting for bombs and orders. In these *Complex* nights we three drink the champagne uncle sends now and then as well, and my hand unexpectedly runs up aunt's French silk stockings; thin dresses with lots of buttons go with them, they allow "inchmeal enjoyment," I explain to her, she's continually being amazed at me. She shouldn't have brought me Goethe's *Faust*, either, but today, with Granma guaranteeing me at least three hours deathly hush, I grab *The Psychology of Women* with its spicy confessions, to add a few new particulars to the good old facts of life. The familiar parental room empty, transformed: boy's room, naughty boy's room, stifling green May air and warm blue flooding through all the openings into the other rooms, the grown-up world a fairy tale recently discovered, the grown-ups rejuvenated, all those tedious old — or so you thought — mentors, grouches, spoilsports, men and women alike, turn out to be panty-merchants, parental homes love nests, offices and factories brothels. And here we are, just about to jump aboard, tired of children's games and learning and behaving ourselves, boys on our way up and the — from that perspective — delightful girls on the other side of the wall in the schools. I sit there fidgeting, and discover, as a bonus, precisely how to trigger off the reflex that has already sometimes confused and wetted me climbing the pole; I test it out, right through to the end and, nothing but gratitude, enter the required data in my experiment notebook, along with my prismas and lenses with their focal length, moon rings observed and spectra. It is well known that every experiment should be set down in such a way that it can be repeated. In all my talentless ineptitude, but also in all my continuing this-is-just-the-beginning joy, I even let my hormones (as I've just discovered) dictate a poem to "my girl" — if only I had one! Hodler, our trailblazer in these things, is in for a surprise at our next rummy session.

February '43   Episode 37
Eichgraben, Vienna Woods. Coal shovel hisses, glows a stinging, nose-tingling red; bites into broad, black stick, melts it, hickory fumes rising from the smear of scorch-marks on the rosy plank, You crazy or sumthin'? Never waxed a ski before? Sufferin' cowshit! Stomach-turning, the tiny village down below, in freefall, unstoppable, the unpracticed elongated feet sensing every grain of the nutty, milky snow that never stops falling, his mouth gulps a hurricane, everything they've been taught becomes impetus, impact, trauma, the five pillage the hut, the cigarettes turn into gigantic sticks of ash, the ash sucks greedily into the schnapps, homemade by Balagyi, the crushed-up antipyrine tablets are supposed to make you even more horny, you chump, you get more drunk, but you can't get it up, a girl, oh for a girl, d'you remember, Kurti, when we burnt our hands (the trial of courage in the shithouse), now it's the winter howling outside, only 20 kilometers outside Vienna, but foreign weather, a city death won't give us this lovely frisson any more, the winter, hardening the snow into glass that slices you open at a touch, I feel sick, d'you hear, I'm gonna throw up; On my blanket? You outta your mind or what? Say that again, just say my homemade hooch's crap again!; Crap from the whorehouse can! blows, blood, black eyes. Boy, were we crazy, eh? Fantastic!

January '43   Episode 38
Rummy. Vitrov has a new place where he belongs: the

rummy game. This card game's sometimes called idiot's poker, but they don't care. Back in Vienna, his tormentors from the camp on the Kamp have been transformed into a card school. A school, and he can't get there quick enough! They play in Mother Hodler's pale tenement kitchen, on a peeling white, wibble-wobble table covered in oilcloth with the surface flaking off, helped, here and there, by a bored knife. They don't only *buy* and *go out,* they also drink ersatz coffee with a little saccharine — Hodler's mother is a kindly woman. When they get three jokers in their hand they give a silent squeal of joy. They could play for a hundred hours, do it for eight at the most. It's just the rest of life that's boring. D'you think we can hold onto Stalingrad? asks Paviani. Definitely, says Vitrov. But Africa's lost, says Wulsch. From Tunis we'll drive them all into the sea, says Vitrov. Attaboy! roars Hodler, thumping Vitrov on the shoulder. He's a petty officer in the naval section of the Hitler Youth and although Viennese through and through, he likes to play the northern sea-dog. Paviani and Wulsch, his vassals, sit up straight and believe in the final victory, if they get dealt enough jokers. The cards Vitrov made himself from cardboard, so he can play rummy at home, with Mama, don't have the magic of the genuine, stiffly laquered, chalk-powdered ones. The fresh bubbling pot of coffee substitute arrives. Yellow, with orange spots. He completes one set in his hand. Frau Hodler, gray and kindly. To belong to the card school he has to forget his specially made pack, descend from the glorious heights of solitude to the happy levels of little games they play to drive away the boredom of waiting together at the army transport depot before they're sent their separate ways to the front.

1 January 43   **Episode 39**
New Year's visit to Balagyi's. Still sitting out the old year. Windows in mourning: the heavy slats of unfinished wood keeping the paper of the black-out blinds taut. But playing with Christmas presents (there were some!). Battle chess with Papa (his presence a special present): burgundy red and somber blue bakelite: tanks, bombs, grenades, soldiers; tanks can only move in a *straight* line. Mama distracts, putting down and talking about all the colorful little figures sold in aid of the Winter Relief Fund by the collecting-box boys over several years. Now all belong to the sonandheir. Who, with the unfeeling punctuality of poultry, has laid his New Year poem full of gratitude to his parents and hopes for better times to come. With confidence in victory as an obligatory ingredient. Then he sits in the even darker corner reading some unsuspectingly instructive material. From Dr. Bičovski's New Year present: a doctor's desk diary for the year that's just past, unwritten on and with the coming year at the back, tomorrow Mama's going to stick the pile of new recipes in, blancmange made with water, mock roasts of oatmeal and pumpkin, ersatz wine from apple cores and yeast, rye-flour cakes with saccharine and punch flavorings. For the moment the following is still legible:

January 3, 1912 — Felix Dahn died. January 9, 1927 — Houston Stewart Chamberlain died. Chamberlain?! January 15, 1933 — NSDAP victorious in Lippe election. January 20, 1943 — Act for the Organization of Labor. *Women's attractions* have a double purpose. All the attractions for the man that the woman brings to their marriage benefit the child. *Work and a high birth rate.* The efforts made by National Socialism to increase the birth rate will also help improve the genetic pool since experience has shown that a reduction in the number of births tends to exhaust the natural supply of sound genetic material. February 7, 1915 — Winter Battle of the Masurian Lakes. February 10, 1920 — Plebiscite in

North Schleswig. February 11, 1927 — Meeting Hall battle aha in the Pharus Halls in Berlin, first engagement in the fight for Berlin. February 13, 1883 — Richard Wagner died. February 17, 1940 — Eng. attack on the *Altmark* in Norwegian territorial waters. February 21, 1916 — Start of Battle of Verdun. *Mothers, the key to the nation's future.* The health of a nation depends entirely on how much its women are prepared to put into being good mothers. It behooves us, therefore, to set our mothers on pedestals, and our men must look up to them in awe. Before it can become a powerful fatherland, Germany must first be a fruitful land of mothers and children. Women too, as the Führer emphasized in Nuremberg in 1935, have their own battlefield. Every child they bear for the nation is a blow in their own fight for the nation. Man's concern is the people, woman's the family. *The reception of the spermatozoa* in the uterus takes 3 minutes when the woman experiences orgasm; they are drawn up by the contraction of the uterus during orgasm. When orgasm does not take place the spermatozoa need about an hour to make their way up into the uterus. Orgasm is thus of great importance for successful conception. February 28, 1833 — Chief of General Staff Count v. Schlieffen born. March 2, 1680 — French devastate Heidelberg. March 6, 1930 — Admiral of the Fleet v. Tirpitz died. March 7, 1936 — reestablishment of German military sovereignty in the Rhineland. March 10, 1813 — Iron Cross instituted. *Late marriage means the loss of a generation.* In terms of population growth, the negative effect of so-called late marriage is usually accounted for by the fact that such marriages seldom produce the desirable number of offspring (3-4). But there is another, no less serious factor that can be adduced, namely the loss of a whole generation. If in a particular family, for example, all the men marry at 24 and have their first child at 25, then in 100 years that would mean 4 generations and, with an average of 3 children each, 120 offspring. A marriage age of 32, which is becoming more and more frequent nowadays, would mean only 3 generations with 39 offspring. March 6, 1935 — reintroduction of compulsory military service. March 28, 1864 — Storming of the Danish fortifications at Düppel. *It is not in houses with an only son that we find the spirit of sacrifice,* a spirit which is essential to Germany's will to defend itself, but in houses with a swarm of children, each ready to make sacrifices for the others. May 14, 1940 — Capitulation of the Dutch army. May 17, 1933 — Adolf Hitler's first Reichstag speech. June 12, 1815 — foundation of the German student fraternity. *Convulsions (folk remedy).* The child's mind is starting to grow, so the mother must bite the head off a mouse and hang it round the child's neck, then it will feel some relief. *Land ownership and number of offspring.* In the census of 1933 the question of the relationship between ownership of land and the number of offspring was looked at for the first time. For example, the percentage of childless marriages among industrial workers, who do not possess land of their own, was 24.5, twice as high as for couples with land (12.6), and the percentage of the former with 4 or more children — 14.7 — only half as high. Even more conclusive are the figures for farmers where more than 40% of all marriages have 4 or more children. This highlights the importance of the National Socialist policy of getting the Germans to return to their roots in the soil of their homeland. July 5, 1884 — Togo becomes German. July 14, 1933 — Law to Ensure Healthy Offspring. *The love of cleanliness* should be encouraged in children to the point of passion. Nietzsche. *Is diabetes grounds for a divorce?* A woman, who had married in 1925, developed diabetes. The husband petitioned for divorce on the grounds that diabetes was hereditary and any offspring would therefore carry a hereditary disease. His plea was not granted. The reason given was that, although the disease was hereditary, it was not a hereditary disease within the meaning of the Law to Prevent Offspring with Hereditary Diseases. *Man makes history*, woman is history. Oswald Spengler. August 3, 1921 — Founding of S.A. August 4, 1929 — 4th Reich Party conference in Nuremberg. August 11, 1778 — *Turnvater* Jahn, founder of German gymnastics movement, born. September 15, 1935 — Swastika flag becomes Reich flag; Nuremberg Laws. October 9, 1907 — Horst Wessel born in Bielefeld. October 14, 1933 — Germany withdraws from League of Nations. October 28, 1916 — Fighter pilot Boelcke killed. October 30, 1864 — Schleswig-Holstein becomes German again. October 31, 1517 — Luther nailed his 95 theses on the church door at Wittenberg. Wow! Were they enemies of the people? November 16, 1831 — General v. Clausewitz died. November 27, 1933 — Foundation of the NS "Strength through Joy" Association. *Breast feeding among primitive peoples.* In general babies of primitive peoples are beast-fed in the same manner as ours. If, however, the infant is carried on the mother's back, as is the case among most negro tribes, she will throw her breast back over her shoulder or pass it to the child underneath her arm. Sometimes the mothers lengthen their breasts to assist in this by pulling them. *Woman's place is to serve,* and her study from earliest childhood. Goethe, "Hermann and Dorothea." December 1, 1937 — Hitler Youth becomes State Youth. December 20, 1924 — The Führer released from prison. *From the journals of Marie v. Clausewitz.* 27th December (1812). A loyal, loving, childlike character is worth much; for the heart it may be sufficient, but there will always be moments when reason must have its say, and when it must be dispiriting for a woman not to be compelled to *look up to* her husband. *However great the value of goats* for the nation's independence as far as food is concerned, there are so many uses for goat's milk that it is not in any way detrimental to the breeding program if the goat's milk is not used until after the first year.

Goes black, right over the goats. A film running far too quickly, tearing apart in a cloud of sparks: eye and ear close to father's mouth full of an unaccustomed cigar: oversized, a distinct hum and leaving a comet's trail of burnt iron, startling. Been sleeping, Venku? says Mama. It'll be midnight in a moment, come on, up you get. As always, can't stop myself blushing at "Venku." Stupid. What do you say to the Churchill cigar, eh? Another joke: a top hat the size of a thumbnail stuck on top of the broom handle: once it is lit — not without difficulty — it spews out meter after coiling meter as light as a sponge: Chamberlain's top hat, says Papa. Snigger, snigger, the two plutocratic enemies, well-known from jokes and caricatures, both gone up in a cloud of stinking smoke. Are they Jews too? — Oh, Papa, a sudden remembering, why is Chamberlain in the desk diary? That's a different one, the German Chamberlain, and already — That's enough, it's almost twelve, from mother, paling, loaded up with little war-gray sandwiches and champagne glasses — Papa has the book: Houston Stewart Chamberlain, *The Foundations of the Nineteenth Century.* Not badly written at all, would be quite interesting for you young Germans. Look up under "J":

Jews, cont.
hoping for world domination
hope of the messiah
the opposite of Christianity
relationship of Jewish religion to Jesuitism
the Jews' concept of "sin"
basically intolerant
great strength of belief
hostile to all superstition
rigidly dogmatic
not dogma in Aryan sense
anti-scientific
Jewish philosophy: the Jews as theists and atheists
complete lack of understanding for any mythology
Jewish concepts of law
socialistic tendencies
a people alien to us
points of convergence
the "Jewish question"
ineradicable hatred of Christ
usurers since the earliest times
also horse traders
preference for a parasitic existence

That's enough of that reading, lights out, but it's in the bedroom, the clock strikes in a distant room, right on cue the French cork shoots across the balcony into the maples, the slim glasses clink out all the best for 1943; and we also remember our dear uncle somewhere at the front in Normandy.

Now driving along already, in the streetcar, alone, past Blackmarketeer & Son, the shutters down because it's New Year's Day, no! "Closed down because of profiteering!" Papa won't be able to whisper in French with the crabby old cashier — a real lady — anymore, and now the little public houses and factories along the endless gray street between the tenement blocks are already past, the street of centuries of childhood, of children, even more desolate on this day of universal rest.

No, not sitting it out, dropping off to sleep, celebrating, driving past, but in an armchair at Balagyi's, his parents and sister out, everything left with two young people in charge. Like to try my homemade schnapps? Despite his cowardly refusal the offer bolsters up his sense of self-importance: sitting there like two stuffed dummies, two big bosses haggling, the years of small and ugly are over.

Of course, you wanted to see my telescope. "Mine" is good. Father Balagyi's engineer's stamp is clearly burnt into the wooden box, but still. Casually: 200-500 x magnification. (His beloved field glasses 8 x!) Would I commit murder to get hold of it? You should come round at night some time, in the roof garden. But Papa won't let me. The planes. I ask you, when do we get an air-raid warning out here? What's that you've got there? My pride and joy, a separate map for each constellation, and exact! Down to a hundredth of a second. Look at this, the map of the ecliptic! Careful not to spoil its magnificence with my eager-sweaty hands. Come here (after three one-sided schnapps), I'll show you something quite different.

And there she is, naked. "My girl friend." His guest feels slightly sick. D'you like her? (In a whisper:) We're screwing already. (Taking me by the hand.) Follow me. A perfumed room. "That's where my sister sleeps." She's 16.

Photo by the mirror: pretty but buxom. Look at this! Balagyi pulls open a drawer, carefully unfolds a gossamer-thin, dark pink brassiere. And big! Then a pair of panties, not small either, rubs them over his friend's scarcely less pink face, skilfully finds the middle of all middles and presses it against his mouth. Not had it yet either, hm? What he feels is something different from sickness after all. Now he *does* want that schnapps. While Balagyi's away for the drinks he finds by the edge of the mirror a metal stick, a girl's lipstick, oval in cross section, opens it, a dangerous sliver gives off a scent, the fragrance of all the roses-raspberries-liliesofthevalley in the world and of a sweet, caressing fat. It isn't sickness he feels, but like the restless rubbing from sitting on a hard chair.

24 October 42   Episode 40

Night air-raid. Little monkeys were throwing coconuts through the window of the railroad car, it aint necessarily so, but boys of thirteen go more for the Romantic than for reality, ours will grow out of it eventually. A torn black-out blind isn't used to being up at this time, one o'clock in the morning. In fact we're not used to air-raids at all. The blood inside your body sack squirts all over the place in unusual fashion if you interrupt your sleep at an unusual time. The cellar walls haven't been whitewashed yet, the council is supposed to be putting up the Emergency Exit and Break Wall Here signs soon. After we've won the war I'll take my family to the colonies, the lad likes to read futuristic novels set in black land Germany will have. Like sleepwalking, head drooping, even my favorite cushion under my arm. Papers, food coupons, money, all the keys in the yellow toilet case.

Immediately everything seems normal. From now on life goes on in the cellar at twenty-five past one in the morning, you talk to your parents just as you do during the day, even better as far as father's concerned, because he's there. Pity about all my preserves, jokes Mama, gray-faced, making light of the coming bombfall. Granma shouldn't have to go through all this at her age, she whispers to Papa; his reply a sag of the gray chin. The boy's been scribbling again: The Englishman, he says, has violated the daughter of the German engineer. That's not nice, says Papa, should think of something better, son doesn't know what violating is. Enough German women and children have been violated, the boy recalls, grinding his teeth in impotent fury. Ah, at last the nearest anti-aircraft battery has started to boom. But at 1:35, after a brief preliminary roar, the endless blare: all clear! Out of the yellow light. Ghostly return to bury the fragments of the day-night in bed, next thing I know: the alarm clock, horrors of a school morning.

August '42   Episode 41
Leave for shattered nerves. In summer, walking, but in quite a different man-made landscape, oppressed by boredom, oppressed by the inescapability of the mental park, the captive life all around, the wire-netting sky, oppressed by Uncle's sick, peremptory tone, disparaging everything. I have been condemned, by Mama and Aunt, strolling along far behind in their sibling summer-dresses, to hold my own all by myself with this rare relation, this eternal front-line officer, on this tarred gravel. Stand up straighter when you walk. Keep your hands lower down. Those dead flowers should have been removed. Do you see that bird? Damn it all, you must be able to see it! You have poor eyesight. Quivering in my stomach; I wind up my watch to make it go

faster. Then a few meters of silence. The tall, vertical man, released from the Eastern Front for a while, not without the help of Dr Bičovski, who can do everything, stares into space, with an animal's immense sadness. Suddenly: Eeeeyes — left! Looks me chop-chop up and chop-chop down, stares me right into the bark of the old copper beech, I'm stuck there, hardly fluttering. Command: You don't look well. Pale. Not getting enough to eat? I stammer something about Bičovski's supplementary ration card, all the milk and pretty Fini, Papa's favorite, anti-aircraft auxiliary, now enlisted, can't slip us beef dripping on the quiet any more. The clinic for TB sufferers, their hollow coughs and hopeless, vegetable lives, their cheesy lungs and spittle you can cut with a knife, will be even more enclosed and final for me. But hoving into view: a fork round a little hill. I'd like to have a surveyor's table, set it up, take bearings, make a chart of the park with every bush in it. Papa's binoculars, carefully mounted over a scale, ought to do. I sniff the exciting smell of leather, see the unnatural yellow and cornflower-blue of the edges of the field of vision. Are you sleepwalking? Watch where you're going. Have you a game leg? How far away is spring, how far away is Schlesak, things will be awfully empty now and for ever. What kind of tree is that, uncle? Don't they teach you anything at school? A mulberry tree. You can eat the berries. Suddenly he's in France, where he was happy, where he ruled over a small town. The French grow masses of them, to feed their silkworms, French silk, heard of that, eh? Crap compared with Chinese silk, of course. Stupid subordinates appear, puffed-up Prussian superiors, Squire Bumpkins the lot of them; good-natured petty bourgeois; the French with prattling, gluttonous wives; and of course the girls everywhere you go, can't shake them off; one, just a slip of a girl, kept coming to see me, just to chat, suddenly has her first period on my bed! What? You don't need to know yet, but one hell of a stink. You should see the castles, the most beautiful in the world. And massive dungeons, all with the instruments of torture. Thumbscrews. What? Your fingernails shoot off. They drove the women into the swamp! Criminals, all those powerful people in the Middle Ages: princes, bishops, criminals the lot of them! Everything goes ebony black. I suddenly watch where I'm putting my feet. But it's just a dead bird on the tar. What did I say? The Middle Ages? Right up to the modern period! Maria Theresa had witches burned at the stake. They were still torturing people here in the last century. Aunt and Mama whistle from the distance because we're so far ahead. Women! (Corners of the mouth turned down, staring into space.) My counteroffensive. Showing off with my knowledge of the war, my faith in the Führer, "Fortress Europe: from the North Cape to the Black Sea," the legions of all the nations alongside the Führer, even hope for India, enslaved by the English, from Subhas Chandra Bose and a pro-German Grand Mufti of, would you believe it, *Jerusalem*. The things you know! All rubbish! You have to be at the front. Then you can talk. Here, take this. Read it at home and bring it back on Sunday. Not now! Watch where you're going. But all I can see is great stretch of tar. We stop at last, to let Aunt and Mama catch up. A load of crap! War's not pretty anymore. But Uncle! I gasp. You're another one who thinks we're going to win, are you?? Rubbish. Russia's such a huuuge country. Masses of people, more than you can imagine. And the English and Americans have their damn Jews all over the world, financial power, wealth. There's nothing we can do. I believe in Germany, I say, tears in my eyes, which I don't wipe away. Well that's marvelous. Staring into the distance, into space. I read what Uncle has written right away in the gazebo on top:

Here we go.
Billeting officers have arrived. We're supposed to fit another company into the town. Where? We're not happy about it. But it has to be done. We vacate half the town. A few days later more billeting officers. A major makes a personal inspection of the situation. A whole battalion is to come. I point out that it might be difficult. The major starts to laugh. I could fit a whole regiment in here, no sweat. If you say so. OK by me. All I had in mind was to be able to live a quiet life out here, well away from all superiors and staff officers. In my mind's eye I could already see all the restrictions, obligations, socializing and all that kind of nonsense connected with it. Not free anymore.

The battalion's finally been installed in its quarters. Now there are just four houses for us. An incredible muddle. Lots are sleeping out of doors, they prefer it to the crush in the cramped, stinking rooms. That's the end of our peace and quiet. Of the good life, too. You can't get anything anymore. People will pay higher and higher prices. Hens and geese disappear. Here and there a whole pig. I don't like it anymore. Alcohol keeps arriving by the barrelful. Every unit has set up its own canteen. One day a military band turned up, played outside the little wooden church. Hundreds of people. Like a fair. The soldiers went from one canteen to the next, boozing as if there were no tomorrow. Drunks all over the place. Nonstop unpleasantness.

Positions assigned on the other side of the hill. Ammunition brought in little, one-horse carriages. Heavy artillery on the roads, elegant automobiles with generals and staff officers flashing past. Constant briefings for the officers. Damn well looks like war. Music and schnapps. Just like at the start of the war in 1914.

The place abuzz with rumors. No one knows exactly what's going on. One man given hell by a colonel for saying there's going to be war. A few days later the rumors are getting more specific. The enemy, the Russians, are on the other side of the Bug. We don't know what's happening over there. One hazy morning there's a scattering of huge clouds of smoke all the way to the horizon. A civilian tells us the Russians are burning all the villages.

Standing with Major N. observing the mysterious land beyond the Bug through my binoculars. N. gives an anxious shake of the head. "It means war!" Sergeant Klement, from Vienna, who's come to join us, means the same with his laconic comment, "Things're hottin' up."

Alerts come thick and fast. Extra ammunition is distributed, including hand grenades. When will the first shot come. All inessentials sent back long ago. Only combat packs. Horses and carts requisitioned, simply taken away from the peasants. They don't exist for us anymore.

The farmer I used to be billeted with has already taken his wife out to the cave he's dug. They're all living out in the fields. He just comes in now and then to see what's happening. He is very worried. "Sir, it'll be harvest time in a month. No horse, no cart, who's going to bring it in? What's going to happen to us?"

Almost all the villagers have left. Just a few sulky old women wandering round. Yes, it's very hard. No post. We've no idea what's going on anymore. I've got enough to do. Briefings till late into the night. Things start again at four in the morning. Troops are shunted round, initial positions taken up. All positions along the frontier already occupied. No more freedom of movement. Not even for officers. Can no longer enter neighboring sections. Checks very strict.

Shots heard from the woods on the other side of the frontier. What's happening there? A reconnaissance party sent over one night — doesn't return. Tension couldn't be higher. False alarms one after the other during the night, shouts of command, vehicles moving, unparalleled confusion. the longer it goes on the more unbearable it is. If only it would start. And we still can't mention the word war.

Bridging materials appear, sappers' equipment. Mountains of the stuff just lying around. No one can keep track of it all. In the blue distance a lonely Fieseler Storch is sailing round in slow circles.

Rumors and more rumors. Free passage through Russia to enter Persia and Turkey. Russia will evacuate the eastern part of Poland. Those are relatively harmless. The kind of other nonsense that gets passed on simply staggers belief. A casual remark, a conjecture is picked up and in ten minutes it comes back from the other end of the village as a certain fact.

June 21, evening — ready for action. All quiet from six o'clock. It starts tomorrow at 0410 hours. War after all!

Despite the all quiet no point in trying to sleep. Study the maps. Another brief roll call. Material inspected, weapons checked. Contact established with neighboring companies. Already twelve by the time I lie down on a bundle of straw for a brief rest. Our company is being moved to the left, about 4 kilometers, to take up a new position right on the Bug. We've to leave everything behind. Just the men with combat packs. We have to make a detour towards the rear, feel our way over rough terrain. After two hours searching in the dark finally get there. An infantry captain assigns us to our positions. Explains the situation to me. We are three hundred meters from the river. At this point the Bug is thirty meters wide. On the other side, three or four hundred meters from the bank three, possibly four bunkers have been identified. Must be more farther back though. My task. As soon as the assault troops reach the other bank, we're to start building a pontoon bridge. The materials are ready. 20 sappers, who are already in position and know what to do with the material, have been assigned to me. That's all. We shake hands. All the best, then.

Infantry already in camouflaged trenches. Young kids, all of them, twenty-one at the most. My men spread out behind the walls of some thatched huts. Very quiet. No one speaks. Soft commands. Smoking strictly forbidden.

How slowly the hands of my watch go round. 0305 — one hour to go. Will we make it? We've not been observed. Not the slightest sound anywhere. A night like any other. A hundred meters in front is a slight rise which conceals us from the enemy. It's chilly and I'm shivering slightly. I try to check the bridging material. Impossible. Too dark. I go to see the sergeant and the twenty men assigned to me. He reassures me. He knows exactly what's there. Stacked it himself. We talk in whispers.

Four o'clock. Ten minutes to go. I feel restless and go forward again. I worm my way up the rise and lie down in the damp dew. The flats below me, gray-black. Nothing to be seen. Not even the river. Supposed the be thirty meters wide. I try to see the width in my mind's eye. Marshy in places. A ford a little farther upstream, downstream, in the neighboring section, a thin wooden bridge about 50 meters long. 0408 hours — — 0409 — — —

The second-hand jerks forward, it's slowly getting lighter. I can already see the face of my watch clearly. Hills above the river on the other side, just like this side. Only lower. The land beyond them wooded. Sparsely wooded. A strip of dull yellow along the horizon.

Then suddenly — 0410 hours — punctual to the very second: a wall of fire goes up, all along the front. Black clouds of smoke rise hundreds of meters into the air, pushed up higher and higher by the blast of succeeding explosions. Banging and crashing like the end of the world. The earth trembles. A roaring fills the air. The artillery stops firing. The bombs from the first waves of airplanes pound into the chaos. A second wave and a third. They turn. Artillery again. The infantry leave their positions in groups, advance. The rat-tat of heavy machine guns starts up.

The gray wall in the east is getting lighter by the second. A ray from the rising sun shimmers through the smoke and mist, feels its way over bushes damp with dew, squats down in the pale yellow marsh grass. The stagnant water in the pools along the river is a slimy green. There's a stench of decay.

The day breaks in the east. A new world. The Iron Curtain rises! —

July '42   Episode 42

Schlesak's visit. Holidays in the *Complex*. It's not true summer's been going on too long already. With summer-sun warmth: Hey, Venku, Venku's coming to see you today, isn't that nice? The joke particularly tedious this morning. Any friend is a world of his own, and if the current one has been invited, then the boy from Remeti has to remain a ghost. Her and her precise aim-to-miss bull's eyes.

Nervously, it's the first visit between the two friends, he checks everything again: the Morse set for two, stinking nicely of asphalt now it has the new batteries, the marked magic cards, the long paper bag, model airplane parts and bits of wood with patches of dope, still with its benumbing smell.

Schlesak, long missed since he ran away from the camp, was excluded from school, before their friendship could really blossom, empty weeks in the camp without him, weeks looking forward to today — the invitation despite everything — the happy end, the friendship for ever and ever, I blush when I read Winnetou. A little worm in the bud somewhere? Vitrov talking, talking, the wiring of the Morse telegraph — "Why d'you have two?" — blushing dark red and talking, talking, being bright; eventually, from eyes taking nothing in, "How should I know;" falling silent, swinging on the rings fixed to the door frame, now you! Bored, Schlesak obeys, swings just once. Watch out! the hardwood swinging back. Say, could we at least go out for a walk for a bit? So cards and model airplanes stay indoors. They go through the *Complex*, Schlesak yawning a lot. Says which is his new school, sort of OK, I mean. The most attractive thing about the Complex: pigs being fed. What did you say? The pong, you mean? From now on Vitrov will be especially fond of pigs. Adventuring in forbidden interspaces of the workshop regions, purification plant. Schlesak puffing and panting a bit. Vitrov: would like to survey everything, mark in every detail. Eventually Schlesak looks at Anatol, "Say, what was it you invited me for?" Anatol sees in Schlesak the suburban Viennese housewife in her garden plot, easy-going, well-upholstered, much-loved, practical, bloated, heartless... The worm was right, this friendship's not going very far. What's wrong then, Venku, not happy? in a sunny, very concerned voice.

29 June 41   Episode 43

Happy homecoming. Slow train, jolting ride. Seats with wooden slats torture for kids, poorly packed suitcases tipping down towards their heads, cardboard with torn-off locks, string loose round them. Endless waiting. Now even stopped between stations. In the middle of a factory yard: dirt-black graying to dirt-white. Arm of a crane threatens car window, already nearly knocking their eyes out. But eventually the journey continues; not allowed over a bridge; ten minutes, twelve, we're all ripvanwinkling, growing old and beardbristled. Day by day, throughout the decades of camp/teachers/leaders, the children have been imagining the happiness of their return home as rocketing dragonflylike, transparent-winged into the mirroring water, the moon-halo at home, into the holidays, free at last, with all the drawers full of stuff to play with — and now grayish-yellow pears the size of houses are finally emptying their — what, sugar? gas? sand? — onto the rails, but suddenly spanking along, flags streaming, and how is it the kids are all home now? Happiness always arrives after all.

Around 20 June 42   Episode 44
Route march. Still in the children's convalescent camp at Hratz on the River Kamp. We say Rats. We'll be off home for the holidays soon, thank God. Peace for a while from the stupid teachers and leaders with their constant bawling and barrack-square exercises. A hot June day, a magnificent afternoon, but still this lack of freedom. Worst of all is the officer commanding the camp, Termeulen from Friesland, bellowing out his commands all over the place in his strange German, like a blond elk at rutting time. Do they have elks in Friesland? He regards us boys from the Ostmark as subhuman. In his eyes we don't speak, we don't even chatter, we just "jabber." But Bissek, our NCO who's in the 5th year and comes from Austria like us, is no better. And he's sneaky besides, like a lot of Viennese. We have to go on a route

march today, in our heavy winter uniforms, despite the summer heat. We're to be shown yet another slice of beautiful Kamp valley landscape and to practice another couple of songs before we escape back to Vienna.

Bissek teaches us a stupid sailor's song with scraps of English in it we don't understand. It's easy for Bissek, we don't get English until the 5th year. None of us likes English and we don't even try to understand or pronounce the stuff correctly, they're our enemies.

Comrade, comrade,
all the girls will have to wait.
Comrade, comrade,
Goering says get in your crate.
Comrade, comrade,
you've all heard the command
Let's go get 'em!
Let's go get 'em!
Bombs on Ing-er-land!

Now that, we enjoyed bawling that out. I talk big, quoting my father who says he wishes he could see those awful American skyscrapers tumble down under German bombs. The others all applaud. They shout, "Yeah!" and imagine what it would be like. The Americans were all we needed! But with the Japanese and "Fortress Europe" beside us, we'll be more than a match for the lot of them.

Germany's ours today,
Tomorrow the whole of the world.
The feeling puffs me up like a big balloon.

On the slope of a hill we are suddenly ordered to halt, take up the singing posture and gaze out at the picturesque landscape. The slope is very steep. Legs astride in the singing posture, I dig my feet firmly into the loose soil, which immediately scatters in clouds of dust. Your hands have to be clenched over your stomach, the only thing you have to hold on to is yourself. I get dizzy. Knees wobbling, I sing away the dizziness. I have to stick it out through the Song of the South Tyrol, there in the white of June is the little hut with the tracks of my skis, the Silesian Song, now I see "Kienast's Mill" down below to the left, before the next village, as Silesia, my homeland, where a maid is standing by the door, and the song of Marie-Helen, I mean, isn't that the very stream where the shady mill-wheel dips and I kissed her on her cherry lips? Finally we're allowed back onto firm ground. In relief I sing out that my oxhide jerkin's stained with blood and bears the marks of sword and shot, as all good landsknechts should. O Lord of hosts, — what innkeepers have to do with it we don't ask; what's the point, given all the incomprehensible stuff we sing? — we pray to thee, lead thy bold troops to victory.

In the evening would be overdoing it, let's say toward the end of this jolly, full-throated day we polish up making a report. Report all relevant details. Mnemonic: AEIOU: What Where Why Who Whatfurtherinstructions? I'm in my element. Final exercise: when the whistle blows all down the hill at the double, without stopping pluck one leaf from one tree, identify it, report to the sergeant, name it and then step back into line to run home. I get lucky with the most idiot-proof of trees, manage to catch up with the column, dash out to report to Bissek, announce "oak" with my dying breath and finish the run into the flashlight-glow of the sun, quivering, dropping farther and farther behind, bright red and dripping sweat. My winter uniform leaves a damp trail through the hotel.

Because of this we have an early lights out. We look out of our room down at the big, spinach-green rectangle, no longer sun-kissed but still day-bright, calm, sadly calm, but then we're exhausted, don't want to do anything, but we're so sorry for this sad, dying, last bit of day down below, the patch is so closed off, the opposite of free, it grows darker and darker.

One Sunday in June '42   Episode 45

Loafing around. Sudden freedom, unused freedom, makes the camp visible, opens up its inside to the light. Lounging on the gray windowledge: a view into the chasms of the other gray windows, the gray shafts and the balconies where the maids in this labyrinthine hotel beat the carpets. Eternity. For one boy even an eternity without the other boy, without the point he used to look for first of all in every situation. After the attempted stoning and the sickroom, Schlesak has run off. Ruined his life for good, if you keep picking away at the sore.

But from outside and down below the Hratzenhof is better. What, better? Fantastic! The boys say Ratshof. Yellow and full of vivid flowers. They let the warm morning breeze in through all the openings, in and out into the open-air café where there's no service. Balagyi from the fourth year is at the piano aping Rauxl, our musiclown, the way he apes the English, Churchill, Eden and the First Lord of the Admiralty; ". . . . where o where have my battleships gone? — Oh, come now, stop your weeping, poor little Alexander. They're lying on the sea-bed, awaiting their commander." Someone loafs back into the room because the people at home have sent him the music to the Song of the Frisians, he could go on singing it all day, plus a whole shoe box full of homemade potato chips, still fantastic after three days, they remind him of his parents' recent visit and of the Prater back home, today he's been taking a couple of nibbles every hour, full of the good, rich, sunflower taste from the now-German Ukraine.

Loafing around on the benches by the fountain. Lying

down or turning them upside down and riding on them. The girls are already laughing back at the oldest boys, through the Hratz flowers. Luxuriant spring. Green slime in the fountain of course, when will the first frogs appear? One makes his index finger and thumb into a viewfinder to see when he can get the whole of the sun-drenched hotel entrance with the HRATZENHOF sign and the flowers on the windowsills in the picture. Sensation: the Latin ace, he's been all over the world, took a picture recently! The hours-till-food stretch out to the far-off Sunday meal with the Jello, lusted after, refreshing, transparent in yellow, red and even blue. The one with the viewfinder would like to measure up everything and is construing the Nonius he's just learnt in his head.

Loafing around makes everything quiet. Where are our screaming-hoarse voices? Loafing around, the Jello and the second helping in our bellies. Naturally we chose different colors and naturally they don't get on together, bellyache, the world is growing old, tired, sad. Is anything going to happen before the sour institutional bread in the evening, already you can see the boys sitting in the same room as at lunch, with the cold sausage and a sliver of cold cheese?

Oh yes, visit Kaltenbauer in the sickroom. The tyrant is hurt that we go to see him so little. Spends a quarter of an hour biting our headds off. We put up with it, heads down, furious, shamming meekness. We stay for twenty minutes so it doesn't look like the obligatory quarter of an hour. The refreshing breeze at the fountain knocks the humiliation out of us right away, blows away the hospital stench, replacing it with flowers, the insistent ones and the mild ones.

Loafing around in the dorm with your mail.

Dear Tilki,
Why don't you write more often? Have you so much homework you can't find the time? I send my warmest wishes.

Aunt too, you know you ought to write to her to say how happy you are her operation was successful. And Granma was very offended as well, you forgot her name day. Your Papa and I were very hurt that we couldn't even say goodbye to you at Whit because your leaders dragged you off to the cinema. And then we lost the return tickets, ten marks down the drain, but that's life, I suppose. I hope we'll finally get a letter from you in the next few days.

The weather's quite nice. We leave the balcony door open all the time, even at night. No air-raid alerts. Not long ago they were practicing extinguishing incendiary bombs in the park across the road. You should have seen it, it was some show.

Are you keeping your things tidy? Yesterday I went through "your" cupboard. And what did I find? It looked as if the mice were celebrating their centennial there, charming to look at, but a stench of old tar, wax, dried leaves in jars. Why do you have to collect everything. I gave it a thorough clear out, I was squatting on the floor there for a good hour and a half. Now it's all empty and clean.

How are you keeping? Well? Sunburned? Skinny or have you filled out? Is there anything you want us to send you? Don't you need your heavy shoes for going out in the woods? It's pretty bad here as far as food's concerned, nothing to buy. Fruit, candy, you can't get anything, Things have never been so scarce. But it'll get better. At least the garden's coming along fine. The pineapples will soon be ripening.

Is someone doing your washing? It's no go with the soap coupons. You took the old ones with you and I didn't qualify for a new card without you. Have you still got some money? Are you eating enough? It's for your own good. Do you still get a bit of meat? Are you sleeping well? Please don't take too many risks, be careful with the water and don't take doing your duty too seriously.

News. 1st: At the beginning of the week Papa had a sore

throat and his temperature went up to over 100^0. I had a touch too, but we're both better now. Papa's going back to work tomorrow. But 2nd: your aunt came to visit at half past three, with a funny expression on her face — behind her was your u-n-c-l-e!! What a nice surprise! They both send their best wishes. He looks as handsome as ever in his uniform, only very thin. He's lost 33 pounds. The journey took seven days and seven nights. It was a terrible story, weeks by themselves in Russia, lost their way, sleeping on the bare earth out on the steppes, only the grass to eat and vodka to drink.

Are your teachers happy with you? Do you get on with the other boys? Best wishes to all of you. Are you making the most of your time? Enjoy yourselves, childhood will be over soon enough.

Yesterday and the day before we went to the movies. Some nice amusing films to make the evenings without our Tilki pass quicker. I never feel like listening to the radio. There's another big rag collection going on.

Are you already looking forward to coming home, or do you want the time to pass as slowly as possible? There's so much I'd like to know and I don't hear anything. It's so lovely here in the Complex now, yesterday we went for a slow walk for two hours and had a look at the pigpens. They were so sweet, I tell you, I called "Piggie, piggie" and they came running out of all the little doors and stood up against the wall.

This afternoon that slitty-eyed boy from the Jungvolk *was here again to invite you to the Sunday parade. I told him what you're doing and he went away..*

Is Schlesak back yet? Has anyone else run away? How did they do it? If only it were all over. All the women are saying the same. As soon as you know when you're coming home you must write and tell us at once, Tilki dear. Bring the bits of the old broken Morse telegraph back with you, perhaps it can be repaired. When you've finished the things we sent you, throw the box away. And put whatever bits and pieces you can in the tin so that you're not short of space when you're packing your suitcase. Place them carefully, don't squash them in. Be careful with the ink! Shoe polish! Don't leave anything behind, it would be a waste. It doesn't matter what it looks like, your Mama will wash it and clean it up. Like all the rest of us, I'm so looking forward to coming to meet you at the station. But will you go and queue for us again without moaning?

Have a good time, Tilki, and put some warm clothes on, so you won't end up ill in bed again. All the best, Tilki darling, and lots of kisses.

Mama
PS
I'm looking forward to your letter, too, Tolko, especially as far as homesickness is concerned. I hope you have lots of different and interesting things to do there to keep you happy and contented. We're already looking forward to your description of your competitions at the end of May; give us all the details.

We have had four workers drafted from the East in the main plant (one female); you'll teach them German properly.

Love

Father
PS Hodler's writing's a hundred times better than yours, surely you don't have to scratch like a hobgoblin.

Write back that the premature explanation of the facts of life in biology class is a blessing; once I start to get interested in girls there'll be no problems and I look forward to having children.

More loafing in the evening, down to Weinheber's reading. The poet himself in Hratzenhof. Scratching himself because out of year three only Dička and, talked into it, Vitrov have come; usually there are at least five. Podium-remoteness has vanished. Vitrov resolves to keep looking the speaker in the eye, while the latter talks at his stomach and mouth; the type and strength of lighting can be clearly noted, like certain data of a star.

13 May 42   Episode 46

Sports day. The flags will flower their fastest, the flowers will flag their hardest, everything safe, boring, prestigious in the toy castle. Not only that: we're in teams. Lined up. But May, marvelous weather, fit to burst. Lined up to take part in every discipline there is. Even Titch on our team, throwing his little javelin a short distance the wrongest way, even me. Titch's afraid of Grasl, the evil robber chief, though his noose has long since moldered. Even the way there through the aromatic woods had to be an athletic exercise, a cross-country run in gym shoes through the May-yellow, May-green, May-mild woods, Grasl had a cave here, he had one everywhere, nettles nettle our legs, necks, arms, undergrowth stumbles us, twigs pierce our worn-thin pumps, Titch can't go on any more, Kaltenbauer will win the high jump of course, the castle's impossibly far away, Step on it, Antschi! because I'm the second-smallest and catching up with the leading group, Titch's making his fearful-tearful way through the woods somewhere behind, will get there hours days weeks later, creeping, rolling, I despise him, the crack, lash of branches, scratches, blood, one gym shoe coming apart, just leave it there and run on, suddenly with invulnerable horny feet, only the leading runner, Giraffe from the fifth year, is still in front of little weakling Antschi, in the ceremonial clearing where the leaders and teachers are, calling out to me, in the end I'm only fourth, but I'm picked out as an *example.* Leave the weak where they belong, the race is to the swift and strong, I sing to Titch, at the Frog Pool on the way home, are you swift and strong? Immediately a gym teacher's hand on his shoulder, iron grip, Vitrov, do you feel good making fun of even weaker boys? Most wounding is the "even." But the Frog Inn, the frog-wide square of the little town, has been drunk dry, rested dry and we set off into the long Ravine of the Hungry Way Home. At some point or other the thirst for milk appears, it's standing in a brick-cool room, a blue glug from cool earthenware, at last I can link up with Schlesak again, has he completely forgotten me? We're very tired and parched, but I accost him, "Dickhead," is all he says and he's off somewhere, now I'm without a friend, for my whole life until the dining hall spreads us in a wild rush over the seats, shuts us up, the sausages split open, pink in hot orange-colored goulash juices and bedded on mashed potatoes that raven into our hunger.

24 May 42 Episode 47
Whit visit. Grade-crossing barrier. Whitsuntide as well. Hasn't it been decorated? Alleyway path, dusty, a bit twisty at the top. Double sun shining. Greener-than-green greenery. Vegetable landscape, town all around, on a plate, with all the trimmings. Out of the heat into the, well, not quite cool but dark. Browner warmth, milder, stifling enough. But an adventure: daytime annex of the parental home: in Hratz! Unleadered, unteachered, unchecked by other boys, on a chair with a triangle of buddies and a closed door. Joy, joy, stories bubbling out, chaos, trivial complaints, big complaints, mockery, plans for the future. The war, Rommel's Africa. Joy, joy. And then the afternoon!

The Schäffers would like — okay, okay, going for a walk together a drag on what's left of the adventure: the parents, now grown-up couples, go on about their worries, sonny boy silent to his friends. But in the morning freedom was endless, the scenery unbounded, Hratz an open town, and that doesn't go away, no.

May '42   Episode 48

Schlesak. The soliciting party (S^1) has gradually approached the solicited party (S^2) through all the standard stages of intrigue in the social environment they share. S^2, "undeservedly" as so often, simply as a result of his essential nature, as a result of certain basic or early fixations on the part of S^1, or as a result of the structural coincidence of being somewhere or other at the decisive moment, has become more and more the focus of S^1's interest. S^2, for his part, does show some interest in being in this unaccustomed spotlight, but if it goes on for too long he reacts against the fervid and, basically, incomprehensible nature of being picked out like this, finds it somehow or other embarrassing. Now the approach, with the simultaneous and equally gradual elimination of third parties who might distract from or sabotage it, has reached a point where S^2 is prepared to take part in a joint undertaking, which S^1 believes he is justified in assuming will be "decisive" or will "seal their friendship." Without rivals, only minimally diluted by the presence of S^2's parents, which could also be interpreted as a mark of distinction. In this kind of situation one (S^1) is open to the whole world, really *sees* it, every single pebble in the brook, every single hazel tree, but at the same time pebble and hazel closely linked with S^2, like all the animals seated in a semicircle round St Francis as they listen to him. Vitrov was happy.

    Schlesak's parents visiting him in Hratz — do come for a walk with us, our son has told us so much about you, happy, the blood singing through my veins — wherever they go they're just puttering around a cozy little garden plot, real parents-of-the-bride, sorry: Vitrov is Karl May's Old

Shatterhand and Schlesak "his" Indian friend Winnetou, but, in some respects, he's more of an easy-going mare. Today she's particularly easy-going and opened-out, even allowing the impression, as they trot along together, that friendship is reciprocated, about to become a reality. From above flabby jowls and bags under the eyes, Winnetou's poppa casts a worried glance over his son, but momma putterer says, Vitrov's got a bit of color in his cheeks. That certainly makes the greenhorn throw out his chest.

They reach the cold, sad waters of the Kamp and like it or not have to walk along it for a bit. Vitrov, because Old Schlesak knows his way around, Is there a swamp here as well? You two should know that better than me, you've been here for ages already. Yes, but — Winnetou, bosom buddy, allearsandmouth — we don't go wandering round by ourselves. So we're already in the dry, Maymost luxuriant betrothal greenery.

Their way takes them among the deer, partridges, rabbits. At least there's a pair of field glasses to remind him of that, dangling down on Old Schlesak's chest, only noticed now, twice as strong as Papa's beloved Zeiss at home, but without that lovely leather smell that goes right into the lenses, and with a duller field of vision, not so glimmery and yellowish purple, but bigger, like a picture in a book.

Vitrov is last to ladder it up to the raised hide, pale, makes up for it by shaking the wobbly rail at the top. Looks through the glasses far out into rabbitland, now he's Nelson, no legs, firmly tamped down in his flower pot, still keeping one eye on the battle, down into wormy, dungy garden-plot soil so that his dizzy legs, a biped tripod for the field glasses, will grow again. It hurts when Winnetou couldn't care less that it's a good point to survey the land from, Old Schlesak is vaguely interested. Poppa's hunting tales, intercozylarded with Momma's tales of holidays and friends, and spiced with the marjoram of her mild bitching go through Vitrov like the runs.

    Go on, tell your friend, the magic of that word heals Vitrov almost completely of his pain at the non-occurrence of the miracle of friendship, how they shot at you. Terrible, the woman, the things we've to go through with our boy. Sullenly Winnetou tells his Shatterhand how, while he was at home on the 3rd floor doing his homework, he was almost hit by a bullet, fired from the street down below. They're all communists, says Old Schlesak. Our boy seems to attract accidents, says Cozymomma. Attempts on his life, says Cozypoppa.

2 May 42   **Episode 49**
Maiden voyage. At the moment I'm still sitting in school engrossed in the

Information sheet
for parents of children 10-14 (distributed via schools)

In its first year of operation our *Extended Children's Country Camp Program* has brought much pleasure and healthy relaxation to many thousands of junior members of the Hitler Youth with our camps in the most beautiful regions of the Reich. Our Children's Country Camps are not simply a precautionary measure for large cities with poor air quality, but arose out of the Führer's wish to ensure the healthy development of his young people, even during wartime.
Why should your child not enjoy this experience too!? Whatever the parents' financial situation, every child participating in the Extended Children's Country Camp Program is looked after by the organization from the moment of departure *at no cost to the parents*. All that is expected of parents is that they send them to the camps with the equipment and clothes they have at home. On registration a leaflet with details will be handed out.

The length of stay is either 6 or 12 weeks. This arrangement is necessary because we must take the wartime transport situation into consideration.
The 10-14-year-old boys and girls are grouped together in *camps* and are in the care of experienced teachers and Hitler Youth leaders. The buildings which the camps use for accommodation are hotels, inns, schools, youth hostels, guest houses, Hitler Youth residences, castles and other similar premises. They have been specially furnished to meet the needs of the camps with impeccably hygienic facilities as well as rooms for classes, entertainment and leisure activities. The different types of building in use mean that the number of beds varies from camp to camp, but they are always so arranged that not too many children sleep in any one room.
I do not need to dwell on the *nutritional value* of the Extended Children's Country Camps Program. Extra rations and excellent preparation of food resulted in exceptional weight increases among almost all the children here during the inaugural operation of the program.
The *educational supervision* is in the hands of teachers specially selected by the National Socialist Teachers' Association and the experience of the inaugural year was that all pupils taking part in the Extended Children's Country Camps Program showed improvement in their results.
In the camps both boys and girls continue their *Junior Hitler Youth* service. In addition, the Hitler Youth leaders see to it that there are plenty of sporting activities and games to keep our young people healthy and happy.
There is a camp doctor responsible for the *medical supervision* of the boys and girls, who are seen and examined regularly.
Parents, give your children the chance of spending happy weeks at the *Children's Country Camps* where they will have the opportunity of getting to know the beautiful countryside of our Greater German Fatherland in the company of others of their age. *Registration* is through your son's/daughter's class teacher.

My first journey after three endless childhood years! My first unparented journey period! My first overnight stay outside the *Complex* since we've been living here! Delight expectation pride fear worry of course; and of course resentment at the anticipated discomfort and camp discipline as well. But all the arrangements have been made, ration cards canceled, things packed, my parents' advice memorized, the distance to the Kamp Valley traveled, the refuge of the train left behind for the time being, military quarters taken up for two *endless months of childhood,* at the mercy of teachers, leaders, schoolfriends, already the first sour, heavy army-style bread has been forced down, the first morning colors ceremony—on Labor Day with the vicious bawling of the German camp leader: I won't stand any nonsense, you'll soon see!—swallowed, the first open-air class endured: my first picture drawn, my eye even less sharp than my pencil, from life under Richtschädel's harsh supervision, wrongly laid out on the rough gray paper, wrongly proportioned, yet still pleasure that seven blocks of stone drawn as seven blocks of stone and three four-casement windows as three four-casement windows result in something approximating to the building in view, a little grocer's in the town with the shop door and the blind entrance next to it, a little old house, there are supposed to be lots like it in the town, in Hratz, where everyone's called Kienast and about which Aixner, the mocked friend of the mocked Titch, has so many exciting tales to tell, already the homesickening boredom of the first unpleasant sight of the mazy gray hotel courtyards survived, recognition that "now I have to get through this grayness of 9 whole terrible camp weeks somehow or other," and so I'm sitting on the edge of Hodler's bed in the room he'd like to transfer me to — We'll have loads of laughs!

The chubby king is bored. His vassals — the spiteful, skinny toady Paviani and frail jokester Wulsch, who is glad to have found a loud-mouthed but basically good-natured master — are having problems keeping him amused. Ask him, says Paviani, screwing up his eyes into narrow slits, if he knows what you do with a girl. I only know from biology, all cells and teacher-speak; what goes on apart from kissing and cuddling I have no idea. My body has not started to speak on this, I'm twelve and the others thirteen and more, Hodler's even had to repeat a year. So they force me to say various smutty words after them for activities I only half understand. Now the king has a parrot. In his good-humored way Hodler, while Paviani's snarling, Let the stupid jerk die!, explains what some of the words, which I've often seen written in the john or on the blackboard of a bold class, are the equivalent of in biology. When I refuse to show him how I'd kiss a girl, well, you know, the way Papa kisses Mama, he knocks me down onto the bed and dribbles a French kiss into my mouth from his thick lips. The boys are enjoying this. Then he squeezes my bag, it hurts an awful lot. I don't want to move into this room after all, and now I know these thugs I'd like to leave as quietly as possible. But Paviani stands in the doorway and orders Wulsch to help him. Hodler sits in state on his bed and sings more semi-comprehensible stuff in a cheerful voice:

My heart it is a gherkin jar,
The girls the gherkins in it
They're soft and wet and — ooh là là,
That's why my heart's a gherkin jar.

And there's more:

Johann Strauss
And his spouse
Played the Blue Danube
In the nude.
First they lay there bum to bum
And played it on the big bass drum.
Then they turned round tum to tum

  And he gave her his harp to strum.
  They played it on her euphonium,
  They played it till it made them come.
Then he finally gives me a box round the ears. Paviani pushes me to the floor and pins me there with his bony limbs. Wulsch doesn't like violence much so he just keeps watch at the door. The repertory that follows is Paviani's alone: ear-tweaking, head-knuckling, the glove, a wedgie and Chinese burns. Hodler just holds me, well, yes, okay, he does smack down my occasional resistance with his big red paws. They are particularly annoyed by little unexpected counter-attacks. Hoy! And, What?! You think you can—? They are followed by punishments. Furious but powerless, I ask whether scratching and biting's allowed too. That brings me a thick gobbet of spit in my face and Paviani digs his nails in. My neck's bleeding. Hodler commands cessation of hostilities, but subjects me to interrogation. Say that again. You want to scratch and bite? I don't. Paviani: The coward! Wulsch: Just like a Yid, scratching and biting. Hodler: We're Germans, we fight like men. You woman, you! Yid! More spit. I'm not a Yid. Say that again. I'm not — smack. Say you're a Yid, you Yid.

End of January '42   **Episode 50**
The Soviet Paradise. (School essay by Franz Horner, killed in action, 1945.)
  It was very cold for Vienna, about four below, and the next day the coal-saving period was due to start. Before that, however, our class was taken to see the exhibition *The Soviet Paradise.* I have seen quite a few of these exhibitions, the main purpose of which is to educate young Germans politically. This is a very good, useful idea because you can imagine everything much better when you don't just read or

hear about the atrocities but can actually see them as cardboard cut-outs or even genuine objects. We stood around in the deep snow outside the Exhibition Hall, waiting to be let in. We were freezing, but as I intended joining an Alpine regiment, I did not let that bother me. At least it helped us to imagine Siberia, where every Russian — women too — is sent if they arrive too late for work after the second warning. For, as the gigantic poster right outside the entrance to the paradise told us, "their god is the machine." At last we were let into the paradise.

We were impressed by the sight of the slums where the Russians have to live, how different from here in Germany! We saw the dungeons with soundproof doors — they have enough money for those! That's where they shoot political opponents in the back of the neck, and no one else is to hear it. They have car motors revving up outside as well, just to make sure. We saw the torture chamber too, a mock-up just like a real room — how well the people who arranged the exhibition managed to copy it! The prisoners had to dance around on bricks heated by oil until they were exhausted and collapsed onto them. There was a glove hanging up, I don't know if it was a genuine one, where people's hands were kept in boiling water. There was lots of political stuff, too, but I liked my enemies' atrocities best.

Yes, "my enemies'." Together with all decent inhabitants of "Fortress Europe," I will sweep this criminal Jewish cancer off the face of the earth and bring about the true, German paradise where today there is the Bolshevik hell.

22 June 41   Episode 51

War with Russia. Hurray! Germany's greatest adventure yet. It was getting a bit boring. Now we're moving again, out across the endless wastes. We're going to do what Napoleon couldn't. At last we can do something to stop those nasty Bolsheviks. Now all the bad people really are our enemies. Let's make a clean sweep! To the East! To take possession of the immense living space we need for our future. The new fanfare for special announcements. I'd like to be able to crawl inside the radio. Already the map of Soviet Russia is up, it takes in the whole wall, the pretty pictures had to go. Papa, the old commander-in-chief, has spread out the battlefield, Mama, ever thoughtful, has put a thick lining of newspaper underneath so we can stick in the countless red and blue flags according to the latest Army High Command reports. Our line is moving rapidly eastwards, our eyes can hardly keep up. The swimmer, whose powerful strokes have already taken him far out to sea, will undoubtedly cross the ocean. Weeks — and still not a day falling back into the old routine. Victory after victory, town after town. Papa, why did you cry on the 22nd?

May '41   Episode 52
An unexpected day off school. Turn back at the school gate. The joyful instruction. Wild with happiness this morning, even the gray school street is turning yellow and green. Sundrenched the long wait for the connecting streetcar, finally on its sundrenched, airy open platform, heading out into greener, more colorful spaces drenched in the heady scent of May. Inside, we're only separated by the open door, a basket of early fruit — the first cherries? Strawberries? — with the obligatory vicious wasp all the way. It was sitting, unseen and unrecognized, on the grayish yellow wood beside the bolt of the garden gate and pierced my hand with a cry. And the magic path outside the *Complex* as well. It goes, without any turnings, to the street with the cinema, and yet there must be gardens and houses off to the

side: when I was briefly friends with Maxi one summer — that joy at the repeated, unfamiliar entertainment provided — I even knew the way out on his scooter. Maxi doesn't exist. Outside the Complex I see the entrance in a crisp, snowy winter, completely quiet with snow and twilight, and us, the family, waiting outside, some distance away, everywhere in the snow on the right and on the left is the Complex as well, it's all the same size, without perspective and completely quiet and I presume we're waiting for us. That evening cannot have existed.

Into the foliage of opportunity. Mama is May-happy too. What's this? I've got my Miháiu, my Venku. What's the matter with you? Again I go red and redder, Mama enjoying the reflex action. I'm not your Venku, I say, pretending to be annoyed, concealing sadness and the unchaste pleasure at being united with my unforgotten friend from my previous home by the exchange of names, just like the indecent knife that mingled Winnetou's and Shatterhand's blood.

Can't quite make up my mind to grasp any of the opportunities, put it off, buzzing round Mama in the kitchen. What have I done by the time the vertical sun is shining down into the cheery carrot soup? And where did those opportunities disappear to during the afternoon?

Well there was some homework to prepare too. Icelandic. I practiced retelling a saga we had found terribly boring. Hadn't remembered any of it. Enjoyed reading the *Edda* more:

Feasting on the marrow
of fallen men,
amassing their might,
the moon murderer
and the sun devourer,
the foul fiend.

Have you really finished? Mama asked, checking the

look on my face, then in holiday mood produced her treasure, the big, silver-bound history of art, and showed me something I'd never seen before. Don't you turn the pages! Look at that nonsense! We excelled ourselves in headshaking, comparisons and comments. We both kept breaking out into fits of laughter together at Klee's "Twitter machine." It hurt terribly, it was wonderfully funny.

And then I'm even allowed to hold a funny book in my own hands, while Mama, the whole day's over, prepares the evening, with her own hands, her merciless grown-up's hands, she bumps off the most beautiful day in the world. I didn't find the German soldier, who'd always had a liking for Chopin but got over it in Poland because the decadent musician's mother country was covering him in bugs, anything like as amusing as the Twitter Machine. And Papa'll be home any minute now.

Autumn 1940   Episode 53

Field exercise. First field exercise. *Jungvolk boys are tough.* Autumn terrain. The summer growth disintegrated. Terrain: not a park with nice gravel paths, not a wood with nice brushwood paths, but a stone-age landscape to be traversed up, down and crisscross. Terrain comes from *terra* = land, but in a military sense. Land to be reconnoitered, fought over and won by all-terrain boys with map cases, luminous compasses and flare pistols. *Jungvolk boys are silent and true.* Storming up across the leafy hill, the leaves flare-yellow, flare-green, flare-red, and everything all around is something, crossing the freezing wet, splashing stream, calves and knees numb, pulling oneself up on tangles of briers that break off, scratched to pieces but suddenly coming out on the hundred-meter higher contour, the enemy comrades with the different colored armbands that are to be torn off a prisoner long since forgotten, incautiously eating dark blue, yellowish red berries, jumping down into the ditch, can't see the bottom is clayey mud, someone's blowing a whistle, you're a deserter already, and another obstacle, ramrod straight, a hare, mutual shock, across to it, yet like it plunging — or falling upwards — into the safety of late-red, yellow flowers in someone's garden, old man cursing, flee out into flailing arms of enemy comrades there's one on the mouth and my armband ripped off, led away across stumbling yellow reddish brown fields, rich downhill plowland, still in a headlock, to the autumn fire full of thick blue potato smell, but I'm not put in to roast with them, *Jungvolk boys are comrades,* now climb up the cave-bear hole in the quarry I can't manage it already been hoisted up the first everymanforhimself step now left alone but I can't manage it palms backs of my hands bleeding earthing festering shoes scrabble the last foothold away, what's it going to be like year after *Jungvolk* year, how am I going to survive Hitler Youth labor service army *My life my honor.* Terrain's always like that, terrain's always, always like that.

May '40   Episode 54

Jungvolk **meeting.** A big, red-cheeked, rough-cheeked boy, in uniform, comes to take one to one's first official duty as a member of the *Jungvolk*, and one goes red oneself because this awe-inspiring boy, a *Jungvolk* leader, is so nice and friendly. They go through the streets like a pair of war horses, heading for the *Jungvolk* meeting. A brief upsurge of annoyance at being compelled to go lasts till the end of the street. At the corner to the flower-moist, May-green garden plots delight at the evening out suddenly assails him. Then, arriving outside the hall with the crowd of other boys, it subsides to a German sense of duty.

Or: in one of Vienna's garden suburbs, a housing development with its labyrinthine arrangement of white, vine-mantled, vine-festooned, vine-locked bungalows interspersed with garden plots, full of countless tiny alleyways, a neat and tidy idyll left over from the days when the Social Democrats ruled the city, to every worker and his flowergrower, childscrubber mate a fence, a hedge full of lightairandsunshine, the May evening has brought pleasant, still-mild coolness, now smelling more of refreshing, moist greenery than of the countless scented blooms.

Or: at the moment Anatol, on his way from the *Complex* to the *Jungvolk* hall, would give a lot to be turning off down the movie-theater alley to sit in the balcony with his parents and watch something exciting, then stroll back home unusually late through an evening sky filled with flowers and May-leaves, bursting with high spirits, every step a lark, to the quite different, serious green of the Complex, to the conversation of the rooms and a small, concentrated evening nibble.

Even before they get there someone hears a song sung in a beautiful minor key by other *Jungvolk* boys. . . . In battle and triumph, Em A in the van. Most of all the uniformed novice is shaken by the baffling Em A, with a long E, like a foreign girl's name, a bit like "Emma," a bit like the German word *immer* — Always in the van? — and a lot like a secret code. It never occurs to him to ask anyone what it means.

The boy meets with one puzzle after another. One of the others, for example, advises him to go straight home from the meeting, with a group as far as possible, and to keep a look-out because communists are lurking at dark corners. The boy hears that with a pleasurable shiver of fear, the meeting, still a compulsory obligation, takes on meaning, some prospect of heroism. But a puzzle: communists only a few meters away? Enemies in our own country, is that possible? What kind of families can they be? How can they live? Communists, that must be something strange. But then didn't Hitler make a pact with them in Russia?

Or: why do his comrades like singing, "We were lying off Madagascar and had the plague on board, in the tanks the water was stinking, ev'ry day someone went overboard"? And why does the platoon leader say really we shouldn't be singing it? Is it forbidden? Semi-forbidden? What would that be? And didn't I hear somewhere or other that the Jews are all to be sent to Madagascar?

Or: They're taught a new verse to "Brothers in the pits and mines": Hitler is our leader, dearer to us than gold, that shining at his feet, from Jewish thrones has rolled. Where are there any Jewish kings or emperors? And do they pay Hitler with gold? It doesn't occur to the boy to ask anyone for the answer to these puzzles. Hey, let's sing somethin' good:

> Negro slaves go on the rampage,
> rifles ring out in the night,
> streets are full of scenes of carnage,
> strewn with bodies, black and white,
> throats slit open, limbs hacked off
> for the cannibals' cooking pot.

Hey, listen all youse: "Wild Geese," a new verse:

> The Jews go here, the Jews go there,
> those restless Jews get everywhere.
> They try to cross the raging seas,
> their ship is sunk, the world's at peace.

Three, four: — — — Anatol sings along merrily, he can see the funny black rag dolls falling out of the boat. It's different with,

> Land along the Black Sea's shore,
> Beyond the Prut, our home of yore,
> Land enriched by German toil,
> Sacred with our blood its soil —

Germany is calling home
Sons and daughters to their own.
Farewell to the Danube strand,
Hail to thee, our Fatherland.

For that one he doesn't need the troop leader's explanation and he feels somehow sad. Listen, pay attention to the training; if you're good you could become a cadet leader. Too gruesome for his ears the heroic deed of the week: hands burning, still managed to turn the red-hot steering wheel. So 20 knees bend, 20 press-ups done without protest, just the occasional one not done quite properly. I'm bushed! That little weakling Ossi's allowed to stop after only 10, you lot remember, he's got to put just as much into it. Wheee, now comes the best bit. All the exertions are forgotten, everyone gets a turn at being a torturer now; slapping, swatting, punching, pinching, everything's allowed in their favorite game of forfeits, "Polish confessions."

March '40   Episode 55

Getting kitted out. The long gray street away from the center of town, mother and son. And agèd son, his whole childhood is behind him, in another land, another time, scarcely recognizable any more. Now he is ten. Being ten weighs heavily on his shoulders, hunches them. Don't hunch your shoulders like that, says Mother, you'll get TB. The boy immediately straightens up and breathes in deeply the stale air of the small foundries, plumber's workshops and coal stores coming out of black yards and stumbly black cellars. He has just been enrolled in the *Jungvolk*, the Junior Section of the Hitler Youth, the *Jungvolk* handbook tells the new recruit what *Jungvolk* boys are like, what *Jungvolk* boys have to do: *Jungvolk* boys are tough, silent and true — *Jungvolk* boys are comrades — *Jungvolk* boys value their honor as their life. Only fresh dirt on your shoes is honorable. To be cleaned after battle! The summer and winter uniforms. Neckerchief and the knot. Belt and buckle. Corduroy shorts and knee-breeches. The whole rig, plus all the bits of colored braid that may be awarded later, and after the *Jungvolk* trial and the *Jungvolk* oath so help me God the sheath knife too, the dagger, they have to be from the Reich Ordnance Factory and can only be bought in ROF shops.

The long gray school street, where it turns into a bit of a shopping street. Outside the sports shop the boy brightens up. Doorbell, sign: Aryan Shop — all our prices are fixed! Lots of kitsch gifts: painted stoneware cups with Gothicky writing, "Skies may be blue, skies may be gray, But love will always find a way"; "One is one and all alone — one + one makes a home" round the rim of a plate; mottoes for the wall, mottoes for the table; one, under smoky gray glass, the boy thinks is terrific and it's duly bought: "Work is the best play." That's really true, Mama. Once you get down to it you really enjoy it. What a clever lad, service with a prewar smile from the the prewar shop assistant. What, the whole uniform? Let's get on with it, then.

Kühnele, the nearby photographer's where new soldiers, summer and winter soldiers, are eternalized as picture postcards might even make a boy from the East think in Romanian of a dog; his enrollment in Hitler's youngest host and the recording of his enrollment on a roll of film weigh heavy on him, his shoulders slump back into an egg again, look, Mama says, and written in chalk on a long, windowless wall, is:

The Poles already know they're licked,
Frogs and Brits're getting their asses kicked,
The God squad can't shoot straight —
Isn't life great! Yippee!

September '39 Episode 56
Starting school. A long, gray street away from the center of town. Suddenly sunshine pouring down an alley. The new first year gradually dribbling in. High school, first day. Standing around by yourself. A few steps this way, a few steps that way. Keeping to the sunshine corridor. A sudden sally, many steps. Over to the side street. It has side streets of its own, gray ones. With sunshine. Shivers down your spine. One street has a small gray workshop. Barred, broken windows. A gray, yellow sign: STAMPS & DIES. You stare at it for a century. Get back to the other kids. Several in groups already. Hey! You! Titch! You comin' here too? What's your name? Nah, your other name. He's called Anatol! Anatol? What kinda language is that? Anni? Annie! Hey Antschi, why're you so titchy? Must come from Pigmyland. They're all small there.

Right away the first gym class. High gray dark gymnasium. Strange instruments of torture on both sides, up there and on the floor. His arms and legs work like everyone else's. Better than the fat ones'. Piebel's even smaller. Already stuck with Peewee for good. Vitrov relieved. Someone to distract attention. Get dressed. Roars of laughter. They've only just noticed: Antschi's wearing long stockings. Holy shit! He really is an Antschi! And cookies for his recess snack instead of dripping bread. Vitrov unsuspecting, Would you like some? Cookie-nasher! Cookie-nasher! Milquetoast! With long stockings! Stockings! Milquetoast! Milquetoast! Soccer with Vitrov's satchel. Hup! Corner! Foul! Stumbling brawling bleeding. Ears are pulled. Give up! Do him in! Yeuch! Vitrov on the sidelines, glad to be neutral, secretly gleeful. School riff-raff always have filth bruises scratches. Arms folded. What kind of language is that you're speaking? German. He tries to say it with a real Viennese accent. One of the more easy-going ones tries to teach him how they say the word for German. *Day-etch*? No. *Day-itch*? I'll ditch him one! And he does. Right on the nose.

1939   Episode 57
Outbreak of War. Actually I'm the finished article really, not at the beginning of something at all, I've finally, definitively arrived somewhere, in this *Complex* where my father's working now, provisionally as a foreigner, but German citizenship will certainly follow, in this funny *Complex*, which I must spend lots of time exploring now, not the *Main Complex*, of course, but the system of paths in the artificial natural park around it, labyrinthine, curving through the tree wilderness and then abruptly coming across hedged-off ornaments, recesses, even monuments made of flowers, finally, definitively arrived here, where I'll imperceptibly turn into a so-called grown-up, I'm pervaded by a broad feeling, like a farmer in his broadest years in the broadest season without beginning or end in the middle of his broadest acres of grain, at the same time a nipping feeling of love, a roguishly grateful "I like it," the *Complex*, and in love I wander round, in its lush, undamaged late summer, still neverendingly springlike for me, jump through its surprising changes in level, its deep tall warm hot green, still full of May-like flowers, sudden rockfall and tree*top* beneath the tree *root,* and even more suddenly being faced with the kitchen's noise and cooking smells and antswarm of people. Being a child, I'm gathered in lovingly, taken to fat breasts, shown immense soup caldrons, presented like that even the fish one doesn't like, the boiled cod with which Vienna is being northgermaned, is delightful, and the boring boiled potatoes, but then, precisely following the order of the menu, the high point, Bavarian doughnuts sizzling in good, sweet fat.

Gratefully, with a respectable hunger in my belly now, which will be satisfied in our new, still delightful and paint-fresh home with its furniture-shop smell — the woodwormy smelling German-Renaissance-style room, bought for a song from an aryanized textile family who are emigrating, still hasn't had its opening ceremony yet — I abandon my explorations, at least the pathways don't lead to the swamp of my secret fears, but I have to go and stock up for Mama, in the Complex grocery, a cellar shop, small packets of almonds, rice, coffee and cocoa, in case war really comes.

The wireless set's new too, we had to leave the old one behind of course, smashed it to bits first, the new one's no comparison, has five valves, the sound fills the room, no problem, most of all I'm impressed by two of the five, one just has mirrors behind the glass, the other poses as a dark brown plug, but it's still a valve. In the evening home-from-work Papa uncorks the bottled-up voices, Slovaks, Hungarians, Yugoslavs can be heard clearly at this hour, but then, to the ceremonial German march:

True, through sweat and toil
To your native soil
As in days of yore;
Fight with every breath,
Victory or death:
German to the core!

Papa, pale-faced, there it is, the Germans have invaded, we're at war — what will England do now? Aunt-in-the-doorway, popping in after work has the latest joke: Can Germany lose the war? Unfortunately not, now we've got it we're stuck with it. But, Tilki, shh, you didn't hear anything. Why? Otherwise we'll all end up in Dachau. What is Dachau? Papa, putting an end to the discussion: A prison.

I slide into the mood of excitement and self-confidence brought on by victory after victory in the blitzkrieg.

August '39   Episode 58
Adapting. Father gives him a brief lesson on the old Germanic runic alphabet and on the Germanic tribes. Triboci, Vangiones, Batavi, Usipi, Tubantes, Chamavi, Cannefati, Chauci, Tuihantes, Cherusci, Semnones, Hermunduri and Bastarnes. And so on. So that he can understand the point of the forthcoming procedures. He'll need it at the high school too. Practice in the wood-brown of the government department corridor: Heil-Hitlering and heel-clicking. No, don't bend your arm. And level with your eyes. And your heels so they can be heard. The first time they clicked them, father and son, was in the German consulate in Remeti. They're coming to the departmental brown of the door. I'll salute and you say Heil Hitler; we're staying here and you'll be a German boy. The son's head is put in the craniometer. Measured all round. Nordic! The official's full of amazement. His eyes are turned towards the light. The color chart held against his cheek. Adjusted. Blue 3! The official's full of admiration. And his brown hair's even dark blond! You're a real Nordic boy. To his father: Congratulations. But his father gets through as well. The Certificate of Aryan Descent accepts either "of German blood" or *of a related race*. All their ancestors are there and they're all the right kind. Already the son is starting to feel ashamed of their foreign-sounding names. He'll Germanize them at school. Or pronounce them unclearly. We're going to get a family tree, father promises. Pats him on the cheek. Don't forget your father's origins.

After the Department of Genealogical Research, the *Völkischer Beobachter*. Not used to all this rushing around. After the calm of the *Complex*, the huge city. A strain on the boy: agoraphobia and intoxication. Excitement. Traffic: freedom in all directions. At the *VB* offices father, as a foreigner in the know, offers the newspaper compromising photos of certain cross-border fraternizings. A godsend if it comes to war. Doesn't fit in with our line at the moment. But. Filed away just in case. Heil Hitler! He'll grow up to be a strapping boy, a real little German. Happiness. Relaxing with father in the café, before father's first day at work in the *Complex*. Tea with lemon, soda pop. The room dislocated by shafts of sunlight. The funny cane newspaper holders. Father immerses himself in the *Völkischer Beobachter*, son in the *Stürmer*, it's got more comic bits. Mountain ranges of hooked noses, ragbags of shabby kaftans, *peikeles* stinking of garlic, but also plutocratic silk hats on top of gross triple-sponge faces. Little poems about the Jews. Jokes. Their iniquities: dubious business dealings left the North Pole Expedition to die of hunger. A jungle of incomprehensible allusions, expressions. Brief despair: so much for a German boy to learn.

June '39   Episode 59
Ziepp. Apart from the Danube, like a little stream here and there, there's the stream and a few streams, all the footbridges across them, one stone bridge and one arched bridge, and the green green meadows, sometimes water-splashed, and the cellars, sometimes cozy, sometimes the first floors like damp cellars, all green light, slime and creepers; in Ziepp people live on very different levels. And the corner store with the one-armed bandit filled with candy next to the kerosene pump and the damp, rotten herring barrel. Often children around and more outside than inside the shops, and I like to chat, most of all, though, with the youngest salesgirl in the new department store that looks as modern as in the country I come from, where all the buildings are new, yes, I talk to Christl about my country and about the political developments that have driven us out, and about the war that

might perhaps come, and about Mars, that might perhaps collide with us this year, all red, and while I'm talking Christl forgets everyone else until the other assistants nudge her and ask me to take the cocoa and the nuts and stagger back out into the white dust of the blindingly hot morning street.

Apart from that, at the moment I'm baked in a pie with Mama and, just now, with Aunt from Vienna, who's on a visit and seeing us for the first time since those few weeks when she put us up; doesn't she just love little Anatol, you'll see, when Papa's finished filling in here during the holidays, when he starts his work in the *Complex* in Vienna in the autumn, we'll have no end of fun; but for the moment she's really enjoying herself taking a vacation in this little village and none of us is bored and it's not in the least bewitched and silent. So there we are, Aunt, Mama and I, suddenly lying in the grass at the edge of the woods, which give off almost too much coolness and shade, and the strip of grass at the edge is narrow so I lean forward, almost naked, to catch the last bit of sunshine. I want to get as brown as possible, Aunt has lovingly rubbed the white cream with all the richness of lilies of the valley over my skin, but look, there's a far-off unknown hill with blooming and unblooming plants and bushes and Anatol-high wild flowers full of unfeared fat insects, buzzing, adding to the fragrance. As I run, run my posy gets fuller and fuller, but where are Mama and Aunt now, they simply can't be found and I run until somehow I come to a far-off, familiar street, with nothing but newly built houses, still bare brick, red as Mars, it's almost visible in the evening sky again, not a pinprick, but a real red disc through Papa's field glasses with their lovely leather smell that I'm allowed to use, a little moon, it's so close to earth its sure to collide with us this year, even Papa says it's not impossible — the only thing in the whole world that terrifies me at the moment and at least once a day sours the sweetness of Ziepp and spoils our chattery, colorful holidays. Whereeverhaveyoubeenforgodssakelordwhathave webeenthroughyoumustntrunoffflikethatevereveragain and the roast chicken is already crisp and steaming on the table, a whole table full of roast chicken, the room, the evening-sun-lit air full of roast chicken from the engineer with the best chicken run in the world where Ingrid and I, but she's still too small, the engineer showed me a compass now I want a compass more than anything in the world and he's promised me he'll teach me map-reading and in no time at all Ziepp and all its hilly bushy meadowy little-boy-lost surroundings will shrink to a simple bright green patch the size of my hand, and in the thick, white inventors' magazine he lets me read I'm all agog and agape at the idea that in the future we'll be able to record speech and music ourselves, on a film running past a magnet in the wireless, I wish we could already, get moving, you stupid years, get moving as fast as you can, at last Papa's home from work at the crispy table, you don't need to be afraid of Mars, if it comes, then it comes and we'll die so quickly we won't notice anything. But did you know that for the old Romans Mars meant war?

May '39   Episode 60
At the Prater funfair. Positioned in front of all the amusements, the publicity stand for the Anti-Aircraft Defense Service. Anatol stares, his father explains quietly, succinctly. Mother and Aunt groan. For a while after the group have settled down it is dark. Then wailing, up and down: air-raid alert. Pause. The rumble of a bomber squadron. Someone puts on a light in the cardboard houses. Now, like the Vitrovs, the model four-engined plane can see the cardboard town and bombs it to flames and ruins. The

dolldwarves all do as they've been told and go to the air-raid shelter. Except for one, who runs out of the house and gawps. He gets hit by a piece of shrapnel, of course, and falls down dead. Now it's light enough, the dolldwarves come, don their helmets and put out the fires. The wrong way — the right way. I hope to God it never happens to us, says mother. Whew! says Anatol.

 . . . for all at once almost the whole world's to be seen. The colorful stalls and rides, the ones farther away just hinted at by scraps of color, parts sticking up or out, many of them awhirl with movement, a cacophony of noise, from near and far the screeching of people, the blare of clashing music, and the Vitrovs part of the chaos of drunken strolling and shoving; colorful, guzzling, prattling, laden with lots of gaudy objects, the stream of humankind pours into the amusement park, walking on, stopping to look, branching off to have a go, all having fun and the fun echoing back at them from the stalls, and all of this as a whole, all still unbroken-down and the Vitrovs just at the start, all this, says his aunt, is only one of the avenues. Anatol does a jig inside. D'you like it, Tilki? asks his aunt with all the brightness of youth.

Brought down to earth, to the depths of despair: just now we're not going in or on anything, not playing anything. Not until the Arensteins have arrived. We're going straight to the restaurant where we're to meet them. You can look. The restaurant will be green and airy and full of good eating smells, but terribly boring. Anatol is not the least bit interested in any Arensteins, they'll ruin all the fun of the fair, spoil this earthly paradise. Anatol feels a double heartache. Firstly because, from snippets and stories, inklings and imaginings, he's had a lightning revelation that this place holds every opportunity for years of uninterrupted play — and he just knows that this box of delights will be opened only very briefly, and then closed for good; and secondly when, for another such brief and vivid moment, he sees and hears Miháiu Venku beside him — and feels everything again, unveiled, as he did at the time of their friendship and casual farewell. What's that over there? No, we're not going to the planetarium today. Perhaps we'll make a special visit to it some time or other. Now Anatol knows there's nothing else he'd like to do today but see the planets and constellations, created by the magic of light. Anatol cries. What's wrong, Tilki?

Lovely shiny benches. What are Aryans? Anatol knows "Only for employees" from the benches outside the engine shed. We're allowed to sit here? Aha. So I couldn't bring Ezra. Anatol's rag doll, the spitting image of a Galician Jew in full dress: patriarchal beard, sidelocks, permanent hat, zebra-striped shawl, phylacteries. As soon as they arrived Anatol made a yellow star of shame for him, just like all the Jews in Vienna have to wear. Not Rifke as well? The Vitrovs sniff the kerosene-coffee-soap smell of the Lebovics's squint little dark shop in Remeti. Rifke Sarah Lebovics, says father. Why Sarah? All women Jews have to call themselves Sarah now. To make fun of them, explains Aunt. But don't talk about that when the Arensteins are here.

In the green of the garden with its endless boredom and exciting rich cooking-fat smell, the heavenly discovery: freshly fried potato chips. The thinnest potato shavings dancing in sizzling oil crisped to curly leaves, each one different: yellow, reddish, brown, spotted, big, small, air-pocketed, oily, a bit raw, a bit overdone, with lashings of salt, endless waiting in the queue at the fryer and the cash-desk, endless crunching of the wonderful, oil-spiced potato taste, I don't care if the Arensteins never come. Be nice to Inge. Inge?? Her mother had to leave. Why only her mother? Her father isn't one. He's even a Party member. Even when it was banned, that was a clever move. Do I have to call Inge Sarah? For God's sake, Anatol, not a word about all that.

Popsicle in his mouth, Inge beside him, the grotto in front of the trundling car is already glowing red, what more could Anatol want? The mountain's cap flies off. The tiny people milling around cry out in the hot yellow and red. Sooty smoke blacks out the catastrophe. Could that happen here, Papa? Just you wait and see when Mars collides with us this year. Anatol starts crying. Arenstein gives a quiet laugh. Mama asks brightly, Are you looking forward to Ziepp? And candy floss in front of his nose, Inge beside him, huge amazement, Maxi calls Anatol's name from the stage and Don't be so afraid of Mars, you'll soon be able to work out the stars, remember Remeti, and do you like Inge? Bright red face, won't leave the shooting gallery, another six because all six fairy-tale figures have been hit, play their instruments and wobble, and another six shots, one missed, stamps his foot, and another six, but that's enough. The light bulbs? No, not those, that's enough. The tears softly start, but a cardboard certificate, great pride. Inge is fat but doesn't have a crooked nose. Father to Lebovics the last time he filled the hurricane lamp with kerosene: Just be glad you don't have to go to Germany. Your people are having a hard time there. His aunt rescues Inge and Anatol from the maze: glass, air, mirrors all look just the same. The children's knees are trembling. Anatol's boat trip, chewing gum in his mouth, Inge beside him, to a completely different world, evening light, past cities, the other boats, real water all round, steering himself, unbounded happiness, it will always stay like this.

April '39   Episode 61
Noahgasse. It can't be: standing on the pleasantly cool

staircase of the apartment house in full sunshine, all the windows open, the gloomy staircase flooded with both river freshness and spring-is-coming sunshine, Aunt grabs hold of me for the short stretch to the corner shop with her, just three houses along, with the cool, bright, tiled entrance, imprisonment in these brown-gray high city houses yet break-outs every few steps into new districts and to sudden green spaces and the *water*, it can't be — and Mama and Papa and the whole family all together with me — that was three years ago. When I was six. My God, wasn't Tilki a sweet little kid. I don't get heavy legs from running up and down all these stairs, I've just flown down to the tiles at the bottom, to the horizontal, and then back up again —

It can't be and yet it is, it really is today, and today is not a holiday visit to Vienna, it's going to be Vienna and just Vienna from now on and we are refugees staying with our relatives in their apartment in Noahgasse. I've shown Tilki all sorts of new things there are in Vienna: grapefruits and peanuts, and I've bought him a little vending machine which gives out a chocolate bar when you put play coins in. The people in the streetcar really envied me when they saw you and you spoke such pure, foreign-sounding German. At the corner shop I get a packet of jellied bananas and pop one in my mouth. Something else that's strange, marvelous. Your uncle won't be home till the evening, you know. I can't remember him at all. Oh, come on now! Those shelves there, I've cleared them out, you can keep your toys on them for the time being and look, this colored paper, you can have it. How long are we going to stay here then, Aunt?

In the evening mist, with additional contributions from the locomotives, at the Ostbahnhof, the soup kitchens giving off steam, some people get out with us in Vienna, the others travel on for many hours to either the Protectorate of Bohemia-Moravia or the German Reich. Just keep looking the other way, so we don't get caught in the soup-kitchen trap and end up in a refugee camp. We're in luck, our relatives are there and all the kissing and into two taxis and that means our flight into exile has been a success. You can't even speak proper Bulgarian? That's not very clever. Uncle, head up near the ceiling. Leave him alone, he's clever enough as it is. But here in Vienna you'll have to adapt — you're a child, a nothing, d'you understand? The others won't adapt to you. Oh, leave him alone, Martin. Wonderful, resting and waiting in armchairs and the smell of schnitzels. Pity you're getting out here, Tolko, you're a nice boy. Pity he's not coming with us, can't he, Mommy? And in the late, tired yellow evening light of the compartment the little girl in the blouse with red-blue-and-gold embroidery, the Romanian colors, teaches me to sing the hymn, which I already know, properly: Trăiască regele in pace și onor . . . another casual goodbye.

I'm so grateful to you two, I can't say how grateful. If we had to go. . . You don't have to, and that's that. That's enough of that, you've got us and we've got you — From up near the ceiling: Listen, you're family, OK? Come on, you lot, dinner is served.

We spend a lifetime sitting on the benches or take a few steps round the shed. Fresh, yellow wood. We're all getting on each other's nerves. The men in gloomy suits, the women careworn, proud, screeching, the clusters of children, the bundles. What a life, this whole day, the whole year, the whole future. No one does anything, looks forward to anything, changes anything. Screaming and crying, attached to Papa's hand, I quickly pass through the shed to the registration desk where we're deleted, because we have a future of our own. The last sobs: Really no more? Only then joy in this bright morning: we are free.

April '39   Episode 62
First sight of German soil. The train starts again. The Romanian girl and me at the window. Grass, winter wheat, plants unchanged. That's Germany? A boring stretch in the afternoon sunshine. A nice big house there, surrounded by green and flowers already. The train's hardly moving. We wave. First sign in German. Papa, what does Gestapo mean? That kind of police is secret everywhere in the world. But then why is it written on the sign? You'll soon be a German boy, Tolko. You'll learn everything and then you'll understand. I look blank. Are you ready, Tolko? Ready, what does that mean? Yes, I'm ready, Papa.

Harder days are coming.
Liable to recall, your borrowed time
Is appearing over the horizon

Ingeborg Bachmann

Notes

The poem in episode 32 is from August Strindberg's "Attila" in *Historical Miniatures*.

The calendar in Episode 39 is from Gödecke & Co. Chemical Factory AG, Berlin.

"Here we go" in Episode 41 is taken from the unpublished war memoirs of Paul Blaszer, captain in the Engineer Corps: *Vom Atlantik bis an die Wolga*.

Andreas Okopenko

Reflections on a new edition of *Child Nazi*

The reception of the earlier edition of this novel suggested I should append two explanatory statements to the new edition.

1. I have not always stuck to the language of the child, but I have kept to his range of physical and mental experience. I felt it would have been too easy to present my experiences of those times *in retrospect*, from the knowledge and standpoint of what a grown-up, who is a passionate democrat, who has learned, that is, looking down from the elevated perspective of one who knows it all because he knows it today. The political and moral message of the book, which is not in the least concealed, which is quite open, is contained in the selection and montage of the episodes. I have repeatedly chosen scenes and extracts which make clear the indoctrination, the manipulation reaching into the details of everyday life and the romanticism of puberty, the unquestioning acceptance of everything by the young people of the time and an ethos emphasizing national, "hard," warlike virtues, almost an atmosphere of military law.

2. Anatol Vitrov is not a one-to-one portrait of me. This is not an autobiographical novel, nor a *roman à clef*. It is authentic insofar as the extracts from diaries and newspapers are concerned, the historical events and the vocabulary of the time. Also authentic are the atmosphere and the scenes characteristic of that state and of a young boy at that time, the first inklings of love and sex. But his parents, their lives, their characters, the region they have come from to Vienna, the complex where Anatol's father works are kept deliberately vague, unspecific. It is not Okopenko who is the

hero of the book, not even Anatol, really. It is not without reason that I vary the figure the "I" refers to in the course of the narrative, often even within individual episodes; now the "I" is the boy who teases the girls, now the girl he is tormenting, now the boastful boy, now the clever one, once even the landscape observing Anatol in his wanderings, and not vice versa. I will perhaps attempt to tell my own life story and my father's probably more interesting real life, in an old man's memoirs, but I haven't done so in *Child Nazi*.

Andreas Okopenko

AFTERWORD

"Anatol Vitrov is not a one-to-one portrait of me. This is not an autobiographical novel. . . ." Okopenko felt compelled to add this note to the second edition of *Child Nazi* after his experiences with the reception of the first. His disclaimer notwithstanding, there are close parallels between Okopenko and the central figure of *Child Nazi* — which readers are encouraged to bear in mind through the picture of a rather wan-looking young Okopenko in Hitler Youth uniform on the cover of both German editions. Andreas Okopenko was born in 1930 into a German-speaking family in Kaschau, now Košice in eastern Slovakia. In 1939 the family moved to Vienna, newly incorporated into Hitler's Germany ("returning home to the Reich" as such transfers of ethnic Germans were called in the jargon of the time). He thus lived through the same period and experienced it from the same persepctive as Anatol Vitrov in *Child Nazi*.

After studying chemistry in Vienna, though without completing a degree, Okopenko worked as an accountant with an industrial firm. He began to publish and eventually, in 1968, became a full-time freelance writer.

Initially Okopenko made his name as a poet, with collections such as *Grüner November* (Green November, 1957) and *Seltsame Tage* (Strange Days, 1963). In the context of postwar Austrian literature, where a return to pre-Hitler orthodoxy rather than any radical renewal, quickly became official and quasi-official policy, Okopenko was part of the avant garde. He was close to the Vienna Group, with writers such as H.C. Artmann, Gerhard Rühm and Oswald Wiener, but later distanced himself from their concentration, as he saw it, on linguistic experiment for its own sake, which he saw it, on linguistic experiment for its own sake, which he saw as self-indulgent and called "mannerism." As he put it in his novel, *Lexikon einer sentimentalen Reise zum Exporteurtreffen in Druden* (Encyclopedia of a Sentimental Journey to the Exporters' Meeting in Druden, 1970): "What distinguishes me from mannerism is that the most important thing for me is my subject matter, not the radius of my peacock's fan." He was later close to the writers associated with the *Forum Stadtpark* in Graz and frequently published in their magazine *manuskripte*.

For all his linguistic and structural experimentation, Okopenko insisted he was a realist, a writer who recreated a version of reality in his works; he described the novel mentioned above as "a micromodel of the world." He is also a writer who is socially and politically engaged. A critical look at both present-day Austria and the failings of the immediate past are part of his concern as a poet and novelist.

Since the later 1960s Okopenko has concentrated more and more on prose, though without giving up poetry entirely, as the award to him of the Georg Trakl Prize for poetry in 2002 shows. That this does not mean he has abandoned experimenting can be seen from the structure of his first two novels, *Lexikon einer sentimentalen Reise*, mentioned above, and *Meteoriten* (Meteorites, 1976). These are both in encyclopedia form, that is, the material is arranged alphabetically, with, in the *Lexikon*, "instructions for use" at the beginning and arrows indicting cross-references, which readers are free to follow up or not, as they like. The *Lexikon* does have the basic ingredients of a conventional novel in the bare framework of a plot (the journey), characters — with appropriately alphabetical names, from André Anarchique to Xaver Yermit Zeisig — and a narrator who makes frequent appearances. But it also contains a wide variety of other material: short essays, satirical reflections, anecdotes, fairy tales, newspaper headlines, lists, dialogues, quotations, as well as descriptions of people, places, and processes more in the style of a traditional encyclopedia. Allowing readers to choose their own way through this compendium of disparate material is intended to liberate them from the tyranny of a set reading and confront them with "the world." That this reality is, despite the variety of ways in which it can be put together, ultimately an aesthetic construct, though a different one from a conventional novel, is clear. By freeing the reader from the straitjacket of character and plot, Okopenko presumably hopes to free up the connection readers will make between his material and the world outside. In an image from his days as a chemistry student which he uses to describe a volume of his stories, the novel is a "spectrum analysis" of the world in a particular point in time.

Although to a certain extend reflecting the "do-your-own-thing" attitude of the late 1960s and early 1970s and the fashion for "aleatory" art that that produced, Okopenko's "encyclopedia novel" has proved surprisingly fruitful and forward-looking in ways that could not have been apparent at the time. The combination of disparate material gathered together in a strict formal structure but accessed in as many different ways as there are readers has recently attracted people interested in using the resources of the computer to create art. The result is *"Elex"* — *Elektronischer Lexikon-Roman* ("Elex" — Electronic Encyclopedia Novel), available on CD-ROM. It has also stimulated a composer, Karlheinz Essl, to create a *Lexikon-Sonate* (Encyclopedia Sonata), a computer-generated piano piece which is "an infinite music installation which can run for years without repeating itself."

Child Nazi has a similar type of structure, but one that has been used in fiction before. It is a kind of diary, in that each of the 62 "episodes" is given a specific date, the most recent date first, the most remote last. The entries, however, are not in the style of diary entries. In fact, like the encyclopedia novels, they contain a variety of material. The basic substrate, which forms the larger part of the book, consists of the experiences of Anatol Vitrov, but that is interspersed with other types of material, though it all relates to the situation of a child during the war years: a diary of air-raids, a list of bomb damage, newspaper and encyclopedia articles, school essays, a timetable of camp life, letters to and from home, a list of anniversaries and other information from a desk diary, an extract from a book index, a soldier's description of an attack, a school hand-out. The episodes also contain many songs — children's songs, official Party songs, obscene ditties — jokes and slogans from the time. The focus on one single figure is also relaxed by sudden, unannounced switches of perspective, so that the "I" of the narration can also be a schoolgirl, various friends and classmates of Anatol, at one point even the landscape through which he is passing on his way into the town. Okopenko does not abandon the child's perspective, he resists the temptation to use his later knowledge to explain things, but he does not restrict himself to a child's language. He recreates a child's feeling with a wide stylistic range from realistic description to intensely lyrical evocation of mood. The result of all this is a novel that fascinates the reader in several different ways. While the unusual formal structure is intriguing, it is clearly there for a purpose, not for its own sake. What it creates is a vivid, sometimes moving, often amusing, always lively picture of childhood; but this is also a childhood *at a particular time*, and that gives us an insight into the Austria during the Hitler period and into the nature and techniques the Nazi Party used to create a society in its own image.

In the text on the dust cover of the first edition, Okopenko countered an imagined objection to the reverse chronology of the novel: "You question whether one can turn back the wheel of history? You are quite right, of course. But what one can do is retrace the track that the wheel has left, step by step, episode by episode, each one of which resists the flow of time with the power of memory."

Michael Mitchell